DEEP COVER

A Brady Hawk novel

R.J. PATTERSON

Deep Cover
© Copyright 2016 R.J. Patterson

First Print Edition 2016
Second Print Edition 2017

Cover Design by Books Covered

Published in the United States of America
Green E-Books
Boise Idaho 83713

For my sister, Malinda, who was a great soldier and is a fantastic mother

CHAPTER 0

Present Day
Yokodu, Sierra Leone

BRADY HAWK SWALLOWED HARD and tried to ignore the sharp blade held firmly against his neck. Only moments ago, he was enjoying a drink with Jay Collier, an expatriate who'd relocated to Sierra Leone for a job with a local safari outfit. Hawk welcomed the benign conversation, especially after he'd been hidden in plain sight for almost a week. Yet something Hawk said apparently made Collier jumpy—and now Hawk had to consider the fact that each thought might be his last unless he calmed Collier down.

"Can we talk about this?" Hawk said.

"What's there to talk about, *Mister Martin*? As if that's even your real name," Collier snapped as he shoved Hawk against the side of the building. "Want to tell me again about that duiker you killed?" He threw his head back and laughed. "Am I supposed to be scared?"

"I was just makin' small talk, man. Come on. No need to get all worked up about it."

"You think it's sporting to kill a defenseless duiker in the wild?"

"Seems like we have some cognitive dissonance going on here. I've got no weapon, and you've got a knife to my throat."

"Shut up," Collier said as he tightened his grip on Hawk's arms. "I know why you're here, and I'm going to collect quite a price for you."

"I wouldn't advise that if I were you."

"I said *shut up!*" Collier said, pushing Hawk forward into the dusky night air.

"Where are you taking me?"

Collier kneed Hawk viciously in the back of his leg, crippling him before sending him to the ground. "Perhaps I should cut off your ears first, since they seem to be a couple of appendages that don't work all that well."

The sandy soil grinding beneath Hawk's feet served as an ever-present reminder that he was on foreign ground. As the two men edged farther away from the bar, the darkness grew thicker. A small outhouse a few meters ahead appeared large enough to provide any cover Hawk might need, not to mention solving his dilemma of where to stash a body in a hurry.

Hawk staggered toward the outhouse and bumped it hard with his elbow. It was empty.

"Stay with me, Mister Martin," Collier said.

Hawk's captor jerked him back upright. However, the moment they cleared the outhouse, Hawk whirled and delivered a swift roundhouse kick to Collier's head. The man groaned as he fell forward, clutching his face. A hit to the throat and two more powerful kicks to the ribs—one crackled like a fire fueled by green wood—and Collier was done. Hawk punched his assailant in the face, knocking him out.

In a way, Hawk felt sorry for the man, saddened over the fact that his path had come to an end. *Wrong time, wrong place.* But it was an easy call—him or this expat who was about to kill him or worse: out him to a local terrorist. Grabbing the man by the nape of his neck, Hawk positioned himself behind Collier—and twisted until he heard a *crack*. Hawk picked up Collier's limp body and moved it into the outhouse. Once he situated Collier on the toilet, Hawk slit Collier's wrist so he began to bleed out. It'd look like a suicide—and no local law enforcement was going to think twice about looking into the death of an obnoxious American, even if the circumstances seemed odd.

Hawk was almost through the door when he stopped and turned back to look at Collier. The blood dripped hard and fast from his wrist and onto the dirt floor.

He wouldn't be the last person Hawk would kill on this mission. He had a job to do, and there was no margin for error.

CHAPTER 1

Two weeks earlier
Lake Anna, Virginia

HAWK YANKED ON HIS FISHING ROD and started to wrestle with what he initially believed to be a fish. But after a few moments, it was painfully obvious that he'd snagged his line on some debris. It'd been nearly fifty years since Virginia's power company flooded the area to cool the nearby nuclear power plant—and there was still plenty of garbage along the lakebed.

He whipped his rod back and forth for a few seconds in an effort to free the line before it snapped. Hawk snarled as he reeled in the rest of the twine and then rummaged through his tackle box for another weight and lure. Behind him, a slow clap began. But he didn't have to turn his head. The cigar smoke gave away his visitor two minutes earlier.

"Blunt," Hawk said, his back still turned to the senator. "What are you doing here?" He bit hard on his fishing line, severing it before threading the line through a new weight.

Maintaining a deliberate stride, Blunt continued toward him with heavy footfalls on the dock echoing off the water.

Hawk stopped his repair work and looked over his shoulder, glaring at Blunt. "I think I asked you a question."

Blunt came to a stop about a meter away from Hawk. "Questions don't always deserve answers."

"Mine do. At least, if you want me to keep working for you, they do."

Blunt pulled the cigar out of his mouth and stared out across the lake. Fishing boats and jet skis dotted the glassy water, the hum of the motors barely audible from the dock. On the horizon, the sun was slipping away for the evening.

"These people have no freakin' idea how good they've got it," Blunt said before stuffing his cigar back in his mouth. "They're livin' a fairy tale thanks to people like me and you."

Hawk stood up and stared Blunt in the eyes. "What do you want?"

Blunt turned his back on Hawk and sauntered down the dock. "Same thing as you, I suppose—world peace, a big bank account." He paused. "Power."

Hawk tightened his fishing line and returned his attention to Blunt. "We don't share the same ambitions."

"That's a shame, Hawk. That's a damn shame. I thought you were gonna be my guy for a long time."

"Excuse me for not returning your affinity," Hawk growled. "That's kind of how I am when people lie to me."

"Who's lying to you, Hawk?"

"Don't play games with me. You know good and well that you've hidden the truth from me."

"Hiding is not the same as lying."

"It is when you let me believe a lie—especially since it had to do with who my father really was. The fact that you allowed me to believe that Tom Colton, the U.S. military's most revered weapons maker, was my father makes you one twisted man. Every kid should know his father—at least know who he is."

Blunt slowly raised his eyebrows and nodded. "I figured you'd eventually find out one day."

Hawk huffed. "Helluva way to build trust. Just let the sucker discover it on his own."

Blunt took the cigar out of his mouth and blew several rings. "However you may feel about what I did, just know that I was protecting you."

"Protecting me? From the truth?"

"If you ever get to be in a position like mine, you'll quickly learn that achieving success on a mission is far more important than making sure everybody knows everything that's going on. I stopped caring about people's feelings a long time ago."

Hawk cinched his line and then cast it back into the water. "I'm not asking for a shoulder to cry on—just some straightforward talk."

"Fine. What do you want to know about your father?"

"Everything. Start at the beginning."

"I'm afraid most of it is classified."

"What can you tell me? Can you at least tell me his name?"

"Franklin Foster. Your father and I worked together in the CIA."

Hawk reeled in his line slowly. "Partners? You've gotta be kidding me?"

Blunt shook his head. "Nope. We worked together regularly, gathering intel on foreign diplomats and foiling assassination plots. Those were some good times."

"So, what happened to him?"

"*That* is what's classified."

"This is bullshit. It's not like I've got anyone to tell. I just wanna know."

"Look, Hawk, I know this isn't what you want to hear right now, but in due time I'll tell you everything.

In the meantime, I need your help; Firestorm needs your help."

Hawk sighed. "You *will* tell me about my father."

"In time, I promise."

"Fine. Why don't you tell me why you're here? I knew this wasn't a social call from the moment I smelled your cheap Dominican cigar."

Blunt pulled the cigar out of his mouth and inspected it. "I need you to deal with a situation brewing in Sierra Leone. A diamond exporter by the name of Musa Demby. We've got intel that he's working with Al Hasib, bank rolling their operation with black market diamonds now that oil has gone in the tank."

"What's the mission?"

"Find out if this is indeed what Mr. Demby is up to. Secure the diamonds. Lay waste to his operation— you know, the usual. I've already got Alex working on a legend for you."

"So, no school teacher this time?"

"Oh, no. You should have more fun this time around. You're going to be a New Zealand exporter on a big game hunt."

"When do I leave?" Hawk asked.

Blunt took a deep breath and turned westward. The sun gleamed as it flashed its final beam of the day and sank for good.

"In a few days," Blunt said before pausing. "Look,

this mission is a two-for-one deal. We need you to shut down this mining operation, but there's something else you can do for us."

"A favor?"

"You could call it that, but one that will potentially save the lives of hundreds, if not thousands, of people."

"And what does this entail?"

"There were four long-range missiles that were recently stolen from a South African military base, and these missiles need to be retrieved."

"What's wrong with the South Africans? Can't they go after their own weapons?"

"Their special ops forces—the Recces—could, but we believe it might be held by Demby and his outfit as well. This operation needs to be done discreetly and all at once if we want to shut him down for good."

"And you expect me to retrieve long-range missiles on my own?"

"A tactical team will secure them once you've completed your task. But before you go, there's someone you need to meet who can fill you in on all the details of that side of the mission—and even provide you with some valuable tech to help you succeed."

Hawk felt a fish strike his line. He fought the fish for about a minute before reeling in a five-pound bass. He pulled the hook out of the fish's mouth and released it back into the water. Standing up, he turned around and looked at Blunt. "Who do you want me to meet?"

"Thomas Colton."

CHAPTER 2

ALEX DUNCAN ENJOYED TOYING with the
CIA ever since they kicked her out. Her favorite trick
was to hack into the agency's servers and let the ge-
niuses in cyber security follow her digital trail back to
CIA Director Simon Coker's home computer. No
matter how many times she did this, she couldn't wipe
the smile off her face the entire time she was rooting
around in their system for information. But tonight
was different. Even though she made it look like the
hack was coming from Coker, she stopped smiling
seconds into her undertaking when she realized she'd
never find the files on their servers.

You've gotta be kidding me.

She slammed her laptop down and let out a long
string of expletives. She'd promised Hawk she'd look
into the truth about his father and who he really was.
And it would've been easy with the information given
to her. Simply look up the name "Franklin Foster" and
sift through his files. But there was only one file on

21

him—and it stated that all files on Foster were archived in The Vault. That was the CIA's way of saying that either they hadn't gotten around to digitizing the files yet or they were so sensitive that they'd never be put on a server for fear that someone might hack the information. Based on how dodgy Blunt had been about Hawk's father, she assumed it was the latter.

Her phone rang, jolting her out of her dazed trance.

"What'd you find?" Hawk asked once she answered the phone.

"You're not gonna believe this."

"Try me."

She took a deep breath. "All the files on your father are in The Vault."

"*The Vault?*"

"Yeah, the CIA's high security archives, *that* vault." She paused. "It'll just make things a little more challenging for me, but I'm up for the task."

"You're not seriously considering breaking in there are you?"

"Nope. I'm not considering it—I'm *doing* it."

"Alex, I appreciate all you're doing for me, I really do, but that's not worth the risk. What if you get caught? It's not exactly the kind of place they'll just slap you on the wrist and let you go."

"Don't I know that all too well?"

"Coker kicked you out and blackballed you. What do you think he's going to do if he finds out that you tried to infiltrate The Vault?"

"He doesn't scare me."

"Well, he should." Hawk took a deep breath. "I just can't, in good conscience, let you go do something like that for me."

"You don't have to let me do anything because I'm doing it on my own volition. Besides, I'm too interested in this case now just to drop it."

"Just rethink this Alex, okay? Blunt will go ballistic if he finds out."

"Do you plan on telling him?"

"No."

"Good. Because I don't plan on getting caught, either."

"You got a way in?"

"Do I ever."

CHAPTER 3

THE NEXT MORNING, Hawk boarded a flight for Atlanta to meet with Tom Colton. In the past, Hawk would've looked forward to the meeting, mostly out of curiosity. He still didn't know much about the private life of Colton, whose life was lived under the spotlight of not only a relentless media but also one that looked upon Colton's success with disdain. But Hawk had lost almost all interest now. Colton was just another man profiting from war, the kind of man Hawk had grown to loathe.

"Beautiful day, isn't it?" chirped the elderly woman who settled into the seat next to him.

Hawk nodded without saying a word, giving her only a hint of a smile. He buckled his seatbelt and tugged it tight. Outside his window, airline workers scurried around on the tarmac, shoveling luggage onto a conveyor belt that didn't seem to be moving fast enough for one of the workers. The impatient employee bounced a bag onto the conveyor belt and watched it slide off the edge. Tumbling onto the concrete, it sprang open upon impact; the contents spilled onto the ground. The worker rushed over and shoved the passenger's clothes into the bag before quickly pushing it back onto the belt. Hawk had become so fixated on the events below that he almost didn't notice his neighbor craning her neck into his personal space.

The older woman playfully swatted Hawk on the arm with the back of her hand. "That's why I only use a carry-on," she announced. "Who wants a strange man tossing your unmentionables onto the runway?"

Hawk cracked a more visible smile and nodded. Glancing at the woman again, he saw a faint resemblance to Emily, his girlfriend from when he was in the Peace Corps. If the woman's face didn't remind him of Emily, her good nature did.

He closed his eyes and leaned back in his seat, transporting himself to some of his more fond memories of her. Emily grew up in Los Angeles and bled Dodger blue. Every chance she got, she would tease him for cheering for the San Diego Padres. He insisted that every Navy Seal stationed in Coronado who didn't already have a rooting interest defaulted to the local team, San Diego. She once bought him a Padres shirt with the number zero on the back. "That's just to remind you how many World Series titles the Padres have."

But as ruthless as she was when it came to her teasing of him, she was even more relentless when it came to her deepest passion in life: helping others. Teeming with talent, Emily could just as easily sew a dress from scratch as she could fire a rifle and hit a target dead center from 200 meters. But whenever she met someone in need, nothing could stop her from doing everything in her power to make sure that need was met. If government officials needed a scolding, she'd give it to them. If a shopkeeper wasn't being fair to a widow, she would dress him down. If a woman needed help affording groceries, she'd dig into her savings. If a child needed a pair of shoes, she'd make sure those little feet didn't walk another step without them. She toiled in a thankless job and loved every minute of it—until some horrible men stripped the world of such a beautiful soul.

Hawk couldn't think about Emily without eventually drifting back to that painful image seared into his mind, the one where a group of terrorists dragged her away to commit horrible acts against her. When he was a member of Seal Team 3, the acts he was authorized to commit against a Middle Eastern village made him physically wretch. The killing didn't bother him so much, but the widowing and orphaning of young children did. Yet anything he witnessed or participated in wasn't close to what terrorists did to Emily that day.

Her death is why he decided to leave the Peace Corps for good and seek out a position that would wage war against such monsters. He was convinced the world would never be a safe place as long as groups like Al Hasib roamed free. When Blunt offered Hawk an opportunity to do what he longed to do—systematically remove such scum from the earth—he couldn't refuse.

The plane's jet engines roared as it zoomed down the runway and launched skyward. Hawk leaned back and closed his eyes again, trying to forget but determined to remember. After all he'd experienced, he didn't want to waste his life away. He wanted to make it count. And if part of that meant meeting with a man who existed in a strange paradox—both warmonger and peacemaker—and believed he was his father, so be it. The world wasn't so neat and tidy, no matter how much he wished it was.

After the plane leveled off, the old woman tapped him on the shoulder. "What are you going to Atlanta for? Going home?"

Hawk forced a smile. "Going to visit my father."

It was a lie, though he said it with conviction. Only a few weeks before, the same statement would've been true—to him.

"How sweet," she said. "Cherish those moments. You never know how long you'll have him."

"For sure." He forced another smile and nodded,

giving off the impression that he agreed with her. But he didn't share those same sentiments.

Hawk's meeting with Colton wouldn't be endearing in the least. It was all about extracting information and doing something that would make the world a safer place. It was all about doing his job. It was all about making sure that the Emilys of the world would get to fight for others instead of being victimized by those animals.

Hawk's face eased into a smile at the thought of what his impending mission would entail. He couldn't wait to get going.

CHAPTER 4

ALEX ADJUSTED HER WIG and climbed out of her car. Her counterfeit credentials passed the initial security checkpoint without drawing even a slight hesitation from the guard; her confidence grew by the minute. She'd walked through the doors at Langley hundreds of times, but never like this. This time, she was trespassing, intent on gaining access to one of the CIA's most secure locations at its headquarters. Cracking firewalls and spoofing IP addresses was one thing, but beating a building full of spies at their own game? Such bravado required a motivation beyond mere curiosity. With each step toward the front entrance, she wondered if maybe she was getting blinded by Hawk's ripped chest and handsome good looks.

She glanced around as the other employees trudged up the steps and toward the front doors like mindless automatons. It hadn't been that long ago that she was one of them, doing the government's bidding without pause. For someone who'd dreamed of being a spy her whole life, working for the CIA exceeded her expectations—until it didn't. Operations that showed disregard for innocent life gave her reason to pause and consider what it was she was really doing. Concluding that this wasn't what she signed up for, she decided to blow the whistle on some of Director Coker's more nefarious missions. And it didn't take her long to be swept aside. If truth be told, she was lucky they didn't put a bullet in her head and bury her in a Virginia mountainside after the embarrassment she caused Director Coker. If he caught her this time, a bullet might be a merciful ending.

Getting into The Vault required solid tactical planning, an ability to remain a wallflower and unmemorable, impeccable timing, and a dash of luck. Each day, two deposits were made in The Vault—one at 9:30 a.m. and the other at 2:30 p.m. She planned to slip in on the coattails of the unsuspecting curator during the first deposit of the day. That was the easy part. Her most daunting challenge, however, was simply getting access to The Vault floor.

The Vault was located in the second basement with highly restricted access. During her time at the CIA, she only met one person from the archives department who had a keycard to access the floor from the elevator—even some of the curators weren't issued cards. Most of them were forced to rely on a guard or their supervisor to grant them access. But the research division, also located in the second basement, was teeming with employees in lab coats, employees who all had access.

Toting a small stack of files marked "confidential," Alex slipped into a bathroom and dug out a tightly rolled lab coat from her purse. She donned the coat along with a pair of glasses and waited for an unsuspecting target. Less than five minutes passed before she saw her first opportunity.

Dr. Samuel Finkle trudged down the hallway, his head too buried in a file for him to pay attention to what was happening in front of him. Glancing at his security badge again to verify she had the right name, Alex tousled her hair and tried to appear flustered standing outside the elevator doors.

"Dr. Finkle," she called.

He stopped and looked up, his brow furrowed. He pointed at himself and mouthed *Me?*

"You are Dr. Finkle, aren't you?"

He looked around. "Yes," he said as he approached Alex. "Who are you?"

She offered her hand. "Sarah Tillman. I'm on loan from the NSA, working on a project for Dr. Coker."

He nodded. "Interesting. This is the first I've heard of this." He paused. "Is there anything I can help you with?"

"Actually, yes, there is. It's simple but my keycard isn't working now for some reason, and I need to get back to the lab to finish working on this report for Director Coker."

He eyed her closely. "What report are you working on? All of Director Coker's personal requests go through my office. What did you say your name was again?"

"Sarah Tillman from NSA. Look, I don't know why you were left out of the loop on this one, but I will mention it to Dr. Coker. But I really need to get this report finished."

"Fine," Finkle said. Moments later, the elevator door swung open and he swiped his keycard in front of the panel, granting access to the second basement floor.

The door started to shut, and Alex jammed her foot near the edge to keep it open. "I appreciate it. And I'll stop by your office this afternoon and get more acquainted."

The elevator doors closed, and she began to descend to the second basement floor. With only five minutes until the 9:30 a.m. deposit, she couldn't afford any more delays.

When the doors slid open, she hustled down the hall and found an ideal location to wait for the deposit. A small supply closet next to a water fountain was about ten meters away from The Vault entrance. Once the door opened, she estimated she'd have just enough time to hustle down the hallway and sneak into the room before the door closed.

Checking in every direction for other employees, Alex began to jimmy the lock. In a matter of seconds, it clicked open and she dashed inside upon hearing the clicking of heels coming down the hall. With the door slightly cracked, she peeked through the open slit and waited.

Only two minutes passed, but it felt more like two hours to her as she waited for the curator to make the morning visit to The Vault. Then, she heard an intermittent squeaking noise along with a low steady roll. She didn't recognize the man, but his cart stacked high with boxes headed back to The Vault was unmistakable. He fumbled for his keycard, dropping it once before picking it up and waving it in front of the panel. After a second, the door clicked open. He pulled on the door and propped it open with his foot. The instant he turned his back fully to Alex, she dashed out of the closet and walked in his direction.

However, the part of the operation that she believed was the simplest turned out to be far more difficult, complicated by the unexpected presence of a researcher heading toward her down the hall. Alex had to think fast or risk losing her opportunity.

She went for broke and faked a trip. As she stumbled, she slid one of her folders toward the door. It was just enough to hold it open.

"Are you all right?" asked the woman, who rushed over to help up Alex.

Alex pushed herself up off the floor and shook her head. "I think so. I don't know what happened back there. I'm such a klutz."

The woman gathered a few of Alex's folders and stacked them together before handing them over.

"Thank you," Alex said. "You don't have to do that."

"Oh, it's no trouble. Here, let me help you up."

The woman grabbed Alex's right bicep and forearm and tugged her to her feet.

"Thank you again for your help," Alex said again.

"Oh, looks like I missed one," the woman said as she stooped down and reached for the folder that was wedged between The Vault door and jamb.

Alex's eyes widened as she realized the woman was about to ruin her chances of accessing the room. Quickly, Alex slid her heel against the door, keeping it from slamming shut.

"There you go," the woman said as she handed the last folder to Alex. She paused and tilted her head to the side as she studied Alex. "I don't know if I've seen you around here before." She offered her hand. "Mary

Alvarez, head of fiber optics research. And you are?"

"Sarah Tillman. I'm here on loan from the NSA and working on a few projects for Director Coker."

"Sounds interesting. We'll have to chat some time. What office are you in? I'll come by and say hello sometime."

Alex was stumped again. Every floor had their unique numbering systems and she knew if the next words out of her mouth weren't right—or at least convincing—she'd draw some more suspicion.

"Oh, I'm mostly working upstairs with an office Director Coker set me up with."

"I see. Well, I'll see you around."

Alex sighed quietly as she watched Alvarez turn and continue down the hall until she disappeared around the corner. Forcing the door open with her heel, Alex eased inside The Vault and gently shut the door behind her.

The Vault was divided into three sections: surveillance, operations, and personnel. She then removed her shoes and started to search for the personnel files. With one eye in the direction of the curator who was noisily milling around on the other side of the cavernous room, she identified her target.

Foster, Foster, Foster. Where are you?

She ran her fingers along the cabinets in search of the F's until she finally found them.

Ah-ha. There you are.

She pulled the bulky drawer open and fingered the files until she found the one for Franklin Foster. She grabbed it, and it didn't feel right.

Too light. What is this?

When she opened the folder, it was empty.

You gotta be kidding me!

She replaced the file and closed the drawer. Darting down one of the aisles and sinking to the floor, she tried to think about any other possible ways for her to learn about Franklin Foster. Nothing readily came to mind.

After realizing her mission was a bust, Alex's curiosity conflicted with her sense of good judgment—and her curiosity won. She shuffled toward the next row of file cabinets and knelt to open the bottom drawer marked "Ha-He." Opening the drawer, her eyes widened as she found the folder she was searching for, one she'd hoped to find but was still surprised to lay her hands on it. "Hawk, Brady." She opened it up quickly and started to scan the pages, her mouth agape at what she read.

Oh my god.

Rattled, she replaced the file, stood up, and snuck toward the door in an effort to escape before the curator got there. She waited for a moment to open the door, listening to hear where he was in relation to her.

He continued to rattle around far across the room.

She opened the door and was shocked to find Dr. Finkle and a pair of guards standing there in front of the door, waiting for her.

"Unlucky for you, Sarah Tillman, I was on my way to a meeting with Director Coker after I ran into you," Dr. Finkle said. "Looks like you've got some explaining to do—*whoever* you are."

CHAPTER 5

SENATOR BLUNT AMBLED up the steps of the Library of Congress. His reputation as a regular visitor to the library made it a smart choice for a place to begin receiving secret messages from his consortium. If any other government agency had surveillance on him, his weekly trips there would be dismissed.

Blunt remained one step ahead of everyone, even if he wasn't sure exactly how many people were behind him. It's how he got to the top—that and his stubborn refusal to back down to anyone.

While he did enjoy spending two hours at a time reading ancient books or little known historical accounts, he created a randomizing system to determine which books the messages would be placed in. If found, the notes appeared like gibberish to the average researcher and likely would have been thrown away. But to Blunt, the messages were a way to communicate without leaving a trail.

This morning's message happened to come in a

book about Prussian History, a subject that always fascinated Blunt. He enjoyed studying how empires crumbled, a pastime that melded together pleasure and research. To realize his ambitious plans, he understood the importance of identifying all one's strengths and weaknesses.

He pulled out the note and deciphered it with an encrypted code using a special app on his phone. One by one, he wrote the letters down beneath the original message until it was complete, avoiding entering anything on any digital device. Keystrokes and screen grabs were the death of many plots.

Everything is almost in place. Wait until you hear from us again to give the green light on the operation. Agent Green will brief you tomorrow.

Blunt rolled up his translated note and stuffed it into his shirt pocket. He closed the book with a loud thud and stood up. A faint smile eased across his face.

As he steadily moved down the hall, he wondered if he should feel guilty for what he was about to do. After all, everything was coming together almost effortlessly.

CHAPTER 6

A LIMO PICKED UP Hawk at Atlanta's Hartsfield-Jackson International Airport and whisked him north on the interstate toward Big Canoe. The exclusive enclave in the North Georgia mountains nestled in the foothills outside the Chattahoochee National Forest provided the privacy Tom Colton craved when he wanted to relax—or escape.

For Hawk, Colton's estate at Big Canoe was familiar, a place he'd visited Colton a handful of times as a child and as a teenager. But knowing what Hawk knew now, it seemed different. Relating how he felt to others would be a challenge since the majority of people in the world grow up having at least a vague idea of who their father is even if he's not present. Though his name wouldn't be mentioned often, an absent father would at least have a name. Hawk would've been fine with that. But in some ways, this was worse—a lie, a betrayal, a fraud. Yet for the mission's sake, he'd have to maintain the charade.

For the mission.

Hawk swallowed hard and rang the doorbell. Moments later, Tom Colton appeared at the entrance with outstretched arms.

"Come here and give your old man a hug," Colton said as he moved closer to Hawk. "You're never too big to give me a hug."

Hawk forced a smile and dropped his bags as he gave Colton a half-hearted hug.

Colton slapped Hawk on the back as he collected his bags again. "Here, Son, let me help you with that."

After a short back-and-forth tussle, Hawk relented and let Colton carry one of his laptop bag.

Colton took the lead and headed up the stairs, checking over his shoulder to make sure Hawk was behind him. "When I heard you were dropping in, I was ecstatic. I got us an 8:30 a.m. tee time tomorrow at Choctaw Course. I'm dying to try out the new driver I just bought."

"I've got a flight back to D.C. tomorrow at 10:15, so I won't be able to stay for golf."

Colton reached the top of the stairs and stopped. "Why so short of a stay, son? We've got some catching up to do."

"Unfortunately, I've got some pressing business to attend to."

"So, this isn't a social visit?"

"Not in the least."

Colton sighed. "Well, a dad can hope, can't he?"

Hawk forced another smile and put his bag down in his room before quickly exiting.

Colton dropped Hawk's bag and followed him out of the room. "Do you at least have time to eat some of the pork barbecue I've been smoking for the past two days out back?"

Hawk nodded, and the first genuine smile since he arrived spread across his face. "I've always got time for that."

Hawk headed for the back deck, following his nose. The scent of the barbecue almost carried him there. The hickory wood and Colton's special marinade overwhelmed Hawk as he opened the glass door leading outside.

"Now this is some serious barbecue," Hawk said as he reached for the smoker's handle.

"Uh-uh," Colton said. "What have I told you about opening the smoker before it's time?"

"I know. I know. If the heat escapes, so does the flavor."

"Exactly." He paused. "Which is why I'm befuddled over your refusal to abide by rule number four of my barbecue manual. If I've told you once, I've told you a thousand times not to open the smoker until it's time."

Hawk looked down at his feet, feeling reminiscent of his childhood. It seemed ridiculous to experience shame as an adult over a mild scolding from Colton, but he did. The fact that Colton wasn't even his biological father made it seem even more ludicrous than it was.

How can anyone have this much control over me?

Hawk tried to brush it off and hide his emotions, but he couldn't. He'd stared down some of the meanest terrorists the planet had to offer, yet when Colton chastised him, he reverted back to being a little kid. And Colton could see it all over Hawk's face.

"I'm sorry, Hawk. You know how I get around my smoker."

"It's okay, *Dad*," Hawk said, gritting his teeth as he uttered the last word. "It's not the first time I've received a tongue lashing from you for touching your grill." Hawk paused for a moment and stared at the Georgia pine trees towering overhead. He decided to blow it off with a light-hearted comment. "But can you blame me? This stuff smells so good."

Colton broke into a grin. He flung open the cooler at his feet and grabbed a couple of beers. He handed one to Hawk. "Have a seat. Let's catch up."

Hawk cracked open the can and settled into a chair across from Colton. "What do you want to know?"

"How are things working out with you and Senator Blunt?"

Hawk's eyes narrowed. "How did you know I—?"

"Son, I know everything about you. In case you've forgotten, I'm the CEO of the nation's biggest weapons manufacturing company—and we also happen to make some pretty cool surveillance gadgets as well."

"So, you spied on me?"

Colton laughed. "No, no, no. I'm just joking around with you. Blunt and I go way back. He told me everything."

"*Everything?*"

"Yeah. I guess. I know you work for an off-book ops division called Firestorm. And I know you're the lead operative for Blunt's team."

Hawk leaned back in his chair and tossed back half his can of beer. He then locked eyes with Colton. "It's hard to trust a man who knows *everything*."

Colton nodded slowly. "Look, it's not like that."

"Like what?"

"I'm not spying on you."

"It sure feels that way. It'd be cool if you asked me some questions about what I was doing instead of using all your back channel connections to find out. You know, like normal dads do."

Colton sighed. "Do you remember that summer you came up here to visit me when you were nine years old and didn't know how to swim?"

Hawk nodded. "How could I forget?"

"You wanted to use that rope swing at Pettit Cove so badly you could hardly stand it. But you knew you might drown if you swung out over the lake. So, what did I do?" Colton didn't wait for an answer. "I jumped in the water and swam out there to catch you. And do you remember what happened next?"

"I swung out on the rope and dropped into the water."

"And who scooped you up?"

Hawk closed his eyes, reliving the scene. But he remained silent.

"Who scooped you up, Son?"

Hawk sighed. "You did."

"Exactly. I did. And I did it because I loved you— and I still do." Colton stood up and walked around for a moment. "Our relationship might not be a conventional father-son one, but it's a genuine one. You can trust me no matter what, Son."

Inside, Hawk winced at Colton's last comment. He did every time he heard the word *son* come out of the man's mouth. Maybe Colton knew the truth; at the very least, he was doing a great job of continuing the ruse. Each time he spoke the word, it was said with conviction. And Hawk fought hard not to erupt into a tirade.

For the mission.

"I know, Dad. I know."

Colton took a swig of his beer and carefully eyed Hawk. "So, what is it you want to talk about?"

Hawk gritted his teeth and prepared to answer. He wanted to get this conversation over with as quickly as possible, survive the night without any major conflict, and get back out in the field. It was nice to relax in such a secluded setting, but he'd never relax around Colton. Not now. Not ever.

"I'm heading to Sierra Leone for a mission, and we have sources that say some of your weapons have been stolen from South Africa."

"And why are you going after them?"

"Apparently the South African military doesn't want anyone knowing what a bunch of screw-ups they are to let four long-range missiles get stolen out from underneath their noses."

"You think you can steal them back all by yourself? You do realize these are rather large weapons, don't you?"

Hawk rolled his eyes and threw back the rest of his beer, finishing it off. "I'm supposed to track it down and let the Recces take care of the rest."

"Why wouldn't the Recces just handle it themselves?"

"I asked Blunt these same questions, but basically it boils down to their mere presence might jeopardize my mission—and apparently my mission is more important in the long run."

"And what mission is that?"

Hawk shook his head and laughed. "If you're such good friends with Blunt, ask him yourself. But I'm not really at liberty to say."

"Fair enough." Colton got up and checked the meat in the smoker. He didn't touch anything on the grill and promptly shut the lid. "I do have a way of tracking all our weapons. It's a GPS tracker we installed on every bomb, missile, and gun that we make. Nothing can detect it, and up until a few minutes ago, I didn't think anyone knew about this piece of technology. Obviously Blunt knows something or else he wouldn't have sent you out here. We weren't authorized to install it because some people in the military worried that if that information fell into the wrong hands, combatants could identify secret bases around the world."

"But you did it any way?"

"Of course. Those military officials have no idea about how all this tech works, and they live in fear of the worst. I do, too, but I plan ahead and create safety checks to ensure that the odds of a terrorist or enemy spy ever getting their hands on a device like this are next to impossible. And if they do, I'll track them down."

"So you already knew about this?"

"Not exactly. We still need to be notified. We certainly don't actively monitor every weapon we manufacture. But when the situation calls for it, we're ready."

"And where can I get one of these devices?"

"There will be one here in the morning before you return to the airport. I'll show you how to use it then. In the meantime, just enjoy some of the best barbecue in Big Canoe—or anywhere else for that matter."

Hawk flashed the thumbs up sign. "Excellent."

"Don't worry, Son. I've got you covered."

Hawk held his tongue and forced another smile.

For the mission, Hawk. For the mission.

CHAPTER 7

ALEX AWOKE SHACKLED in a CIA holding cell. Her resistance to arrest outside The Vault forced the guards to inject her with a sedative that she had finally cleared from her system. How long had it been? She couldn't be sure, but her best guess was several hours.

She banged on the door and screamed through the small opening to let it be known that she was awake and ready to talk to someone. With her ear to the door, she could hear footsteps echoing down the hall.

A few moments later, a guard unlocked the door and an agent entered her cell. The agent wore a blank expression, unwilling to reveal how he felt about his assignment of handling her. Textbook CIA.

"Miss Duncan, so nice of you to return from the dead. I suppose you're ready to talk now."

Knowing all the agency's ploys were advantageous for Alex. "Perhaps I am. But I need to make a phone call first."

The agent cracked a faint smile. "A phone call? Do

you realize you tried to break into the CIA? You don't exactly get a phone call for something like that. We don't operate like the Metro PD." He paused. "But something tells me you already knew that."

"If you give me a phone call, I won't say a word."

He didn't budge. "Suit yourself. This cell can be a lonely place."

"You can't hold me here indefinitely."

The agent raised an eyebrow. "I read your file—and it says you used to work for the CIA. But based on your responses, I hardly believe it. You know good and well what we can and can't do."

"I suggest you give me that phone call right now."

The agent walked toward the door, his back to Alex until he spun around. "Or what?"

She rushed toward him and lunged at his waist before he pushed her aside. Lying on the ground, she looked up at him. "Have someone call Senator Blunt. He'll vouch for me."

The agent chuckled. "That's what you said in your delirious state near The Vault. And we did. He denied knowing who you are."

"You lying bastard."

He held his hand up, middle and index finger raised. "Scout's honor."

"I don't believe you."

"Miss Duncan, I suggest you take a few minutes

to rethink how you want to handle this. Otherwise, you might be in here a long time."

The agent exited her cell and locked the door behind him.

She rushed to the door and listened to make sure he was walking down the hall. Convinced that he was, she hustled to one corner of the room and fell to her knees. She rested her head in the corner, creating a shield against any camera that might be tracking her every move. If anyone was watching her, she made sure they wouldn't be able to see a thing.

Her feeble attempt to rush the agent was never intended to incite a fight—just steal his cell phone. Working quickly, she pounded out a text message to General Johnson, asking him to send a file on her computer to Director Coker. She included the appropriate code to ensure that he understood she was the one writing. As soon as she sent the message, she deleted it from the phone. If he didn't respond within thirty minutes, she swore she'd be shocked.

Then she waited.

Ten minutes later, she heard footfalls echoing down the hallway. She knew her door was about to swing open in a matter of seconds.

"Alex Duncan," said the man standing in front of her. It was Director Coker.

She nodded. "Director."

He smiled. "I never thought we'd meet like this." He paused. "It's a shame to see you in such a sad state."

"I doubt you mind that much."

He shrugged. "Can't say that I'm bothered by it, though I am a little shocked at your desperate attempt to blackmail me."

Alex stood up, her eyes narrowed. "You think this is an *attempt*. I swear I'll ruin you if you keep me in here another five minutes."

"Give me your master copy of the file, and I'll re-lease you."

She chuckled and held up her hands, displaying them bound by handcuffs. "These make it kind of hard to do much of anything, much less get you those files."

He crossed his arms. "I need assurances that you're going to get me that file or else you're going to spend the night here."

"Like the message said, you've got one hour to re-lease me. And I don't think you want to test me—not after what you did to me."

He sighed and paced around the room. "How do I know that once I let you go, you won't still use that video against me?"

"It's a gamble you have to take because there's only one thing that's for certain: That video will go out if

I'm still locked up." She paused. "But I'm smarter than that, Director. Leverage is only good until you use it."

Coker stuck his head out into the hallway and motioned for one of the guards. Quickly, one entered Alex's cell and ushered her out and down the hall.

"You could've been one of the best here, Alex," he said as she shuffled down the corridor.

She looked back over her shoulder. "Could've? I think you know I'm the best agent in the building." She stopped. "And for the record, it was never my choice to leave."

"See you soon, Alex. And you can bet next time I run into you, you won't be getting off so easily."

She started shuffling down the hall again, her eyes focused on the exit. "Looking forward to it, Director."

CHAPTER 8

BLUNT PULLED HIS DOOR SHUT and inserted his key into the lock. Most senators leaving for an hour in the middle of the afternoon would never insult the trust of their assistants in such a manner. But not every senator ran a special black ops program that was completely off book.

He glanced at his secretary and shrugged. "State secrets in there. You can never be too careful."

She forced a smile and nodded.

Blunt could tell it irritated her but he didn't care. If she ever had the gall to confront him about it, he'd fire her. Besides, it wasn't any of her business anyway how he managed his private office space.

His progress to make his next appointment was impeded by his top aide, Preston, who motioned for Blunt to go back into his office.

"I've got places to be," Blunt said as he shut the door. "What's the problem?"

"Sir, there's an emergency security briefing a week

from today, and the President personally called to make sure you were going to be there."

"Got any idea what it's all about?"

"I'm not sure, but a couple of days ago, I heard some buzz circulating around that there might be an attempt on the life of some foreign diplomat."

"But you don't know who?"

Preston shook his head.

Blunt sat on the edge of his desk and let out a long breath. "You tell the President that I plan on being there."

Preston cocked his head to one side. "*Plan* on being there?"

"Plans can change, but at this moment, I'd say it's a good possibility that I'll be there."

"I'll pass along the message."

Blunt put his hand on Preston's shoulder. "Do you think I should call him?"

"You seem busy. I'll handle it."

"Thanks." Blunt straightened out his desk once more and followed Preston out. Once again locking the door, Blunt smiled at his secretary.

"I'm gonna try this again," he said.

She smiled back.

Blunt didn't make it more than a half dozen steps away from his office door before he was confronted again—this time by Alex Duncan.

"What are you doing here?" he said, his eyes bulging.

"We need to talk."

"Can this wait? I'm in a hurry right now."

Alex didn't flinch. "No, it can't."

He huffed as he spun around and marched back toward his office, unlocking the door and flinging it open. He turned around again to face her, motioning for her to close the door before he spoke. "What's so damn urgent that you have to break protocol and come to my office?"

"Why didn't you vouch for me with Director Coker?"

He leaned back against his desk and shook his head. "I think the better question is why did you sneak into the CIA headquarters today? Care to tell me what you were doing there?"

"Looking for answers."

"I don't pay you to look for answers, Alex. I pay you to handle Hawk when he's out wiping those terrorist pukes off the face of the earth. And that's it. So, excuse me for not tipping my hand to Director Coker that I'm running an off book, black ops program that is operating outside the bounds of the U.S. government and military—even though you kind of already did that by simply asking someone to call me and verify your existence."

"Good to know that I *can't* count on you to have my back."

"I'll never have your back when you go rogue." He took a deep breath. "Now that we have that settled, do you mind telling me what you were really doing at the CIA?"

"It was a favor for Hawk."

He broke into a sarcastic laugh. "So, not only is love blind, it's also stupid. If you have any questions, come ask me."

"Apparently he wasn't getting the answers he wanted."

"And did he ask you to do this for him?"

Alex turned her gaze toward the window and remained silent.

"That's what I thought. He at least has enough respect for you that he wouldn't ask you to embark on such a frivolous endeavor."

"It's not fair what's been done to him, you know. Lying to anyone is never a good way to earn a person's trust."

"Neither is sneaking around behind someone's back. But that didn't stop you, did it? Please, spare me the moral high ground."

"I'm relentless, Senator. *That's* why you hired me."

"No, I hired you because I believe you're damn good at what you do, which is operating behind the scenes. I also happen to believe in second chances, especially for people who are committed to the mission. And part of Firestorm's mission is to make sure that nobody knows what we're doing. You jeopardized that today."

"Sorry, sir. That wasn't my intent."

Blunt took a deep breath. "So, why'd they cut you loose?"

"Leverage, sir. It's always good to have a little leverage."

"Don't I know that." He smiled big. "Nope, I'm still glad I hired you. Now get outta here before anyone else sees you. I've got a meeting to get to. General Johnson has the details of your next assignment with Hawk ready."

Alex nodded and exited the room.

Blunt wondered how long it would be before Coker began surveilling him. Blunt would have to be more careful than ever before. But he was pleased to know that at least one of his operatives had some dirt on the Director that he might have to use in the future—if it ever came to that.

***

BLUNT BOARDED THE METRO BLUE LINE bound for the Capitol Heights stop. During his time in Washington, he'd scouted out every subway station and found one specific bench that wasn't covered by surveillance cameras. The camera directly above the bench didn't pan directly down, while the nearest camera situated about twenty meters away on each side was shielded from the bench by strategically placed fixtures that displayed the Metro map as well as advertisements. When Blunt first found it, he wondered if some spook created this blind spot for the express purpose of passing intel. Or it could've just been a design flaw. Without any major incidents ever occurring at Capitol Heights, Blunt doubted anyone ever questioned the slight gap in video coverage.

Not that he would ever complain about it. He'd been passing and receiving valuable information on that bench for several years and would loath searching for another safe location should some security head identify the cameras' blind spot.

Blunt stepped onto the subway platform and watched his contact make a dead drop in plain sight. A copy of *The Washington Post* was neatly folded on the end of the bench, and the newspaper remained there after the man stood up and hustled onto the train. As Blunt walked toward the bench, another man sat down and snatched up the paper. He whipped it open and began reading it.

Though the man didn't appear to be affiliated with

any government agency based on his attire, Blunt would have to wait. Any move toward the man might look suspicious if anybody was watching, though Blunt doubted it.

Blunt tried to mitigate any tails by maintaining random visits to the station along with various methods of drops. Sometimes the drops were notes affixed to the bottom of a bench; other times it was a written on a sheet of paper in plain sight that could only be read with a black light. Then there was the classic newspaper drop. The only constant Blunt ever held was his regular visits to the Library of Congress. And when those messages necessitated more immediate action, he'd make his way to Capitol Heights.

After checking the monitors for when the next train was arriving, Blunt realized he had three minutes to get his hands on that newspaper before the man on the bench possibly vanished onto a train with it. He couldn't afford to chase down a random stranger and take his paper from him. But he couldn't afford to let the man take it either. Thinking quickly, Blunt scanned the station and identified a box with copies of *The Washington Post* near the entrance. He hustled toward it, glancing between his immediate path toward the box, his mystery man, and the monitor updating what time the train was due to arrive.

Blunt dug into his pockets for six quarters and

mumbled to himself about the ridiculous price of single copies of newspapers. At one quarter short, his plan was falling apart. After checking the monitor again, he realized he had one minute left to get a paper and dash back down to the bench and attempt the swap. He started to panic and bashed the coin release button with the side of his fist.

He felt a tap on his shoulder and spun around.

Blunt laid eyes on a man who sported a scraggly beard, unkempt hair, and tattered clothing. With a black plastic bag flung over his right shoulder, the man held out a newspaper in his left hand.

"Mister, you can have my paper," he said with a toothy grin. "Ain't much in there these days, and it certainly ain't worth beatin' a machine for it. But if you're that determined, I suppose there's still something you might find in there that'll interest you."

Blunt took the paper and thanked the man before jamming five quarters into his hand. "Have a good day."

The train brakes echoed as they screeched down the tunnel. Blunt saw the word "arriving" flashing on the monitor and wasted no more time in hustling back toward his bench. All the people on the platform crowded near the edge, awaiting the train to stop and the doors to slide open.

Fighting against the crowd, Blunt's manners decreased as his panic increased.

The man with the paper was no longer on the bench—and nowhere nearby.

Blunt stood up on the bench and tried to look for the man over the crowd. His dark pea coat looked like the one worn by dozens of other men milling around on the platform. He then started to look for the man with a paper tucked beneath his arm.

There he is!

The doors opened, and a handful of passengers disembarked. The crowd hardly waited until the doorways were clear before they pressed forward as one, shoehorning their way into the train. The man Blunt was targeting stood just inside the door, the paper still tightly snug beneath his arm. Blunt didn't think he could reach the man in time, though he figured his desperation might actually benefit him.

Standing a few meters away, Blunt broke into a sprint. The doors started to close, but not fast enough. Blunt managed to slip between them, crashing into the man. Several people lost their balance, including Blunt's target. The man also lost his grip on his paper.

Blunt knelt down and rose up with a paper in his hand. "I believe this is yours."

"Thanks, but watch where you're going next time," the man muttered.

"Will do," Blunt said before diverting his eyes.

At the next station, Blunt got off and went to the restroom, locking the door behind him. Having successfully switched newspapers with the man, Blunt pulled out the paper originally intended for him. He turned to the crossword puzzle, opened his decryption app on his phone, and started to decipher the message.

Then he gasped when he read the target's name.

CHAPTER 9

THREE DAYS AFTER MEETING with Colton, Hawk stepped off a plane at Lungi International Airport in Sierra Leone. His legend as a well-known taxidermist from New Zealand swung into full effect the moment he approached customs. With a strong accent, Hawk didn't even give the customs agent reason for pause.

"What's your business here?" the agent asked.

He fed the agent what he needed to hear. "I'm here doing volunteer work for a conservationist group."

The agent stamped the passport.

"Have a nice visit," he said as he waved Hawk through.

Hawk stared at his passport. Oliver Martin, twenty-six-years of age, six foot two, brown hair, blue eyes, born in Christchurch, New Zealand. He shrugged. Everything but the name and town were correct.

Three hours later, he secured his car rental—a Toyota Forerunner—and was bumping along the Lunsar-Makeni Highway toward Yokodu, a small village just outside Koidu in the Kono district. Kono was known for its diamond-rich mines. But its location just two hours northwest of the Liberian border made it a prime location to sneak diamonds out of Sierra Leone and into the diamond smuggling capital of the world.

Hawk's final destination was Joubert Safaris, an off-the-books South African outfitter that officially shuttered its business during the Ebola outbreak and had recently re-opened for more unofficial business. With the government urging citizens not to eat bush meat, the bay duiker population surged in some parts of the country. They had reportedly begun roaming the streets and were becoming a nuisance in some of the smaller villages, and Joubert Safaris secured unofficial permission to round up several dozen and hand them over to conservation groups to be dissected and studied.

Only Hawk wasn't presenting himself as a conservationist to anyone else. From here on out, he was Oliver Martin, Kiwi taxidermist and hunting enthusiast.

After an hour of rumbling along Sierra Leone's poor excuse of a highway, he called Alex on his satellite phone. The six-hour time difference meant she might be in a better mood than when he'd called her from the Middle East.

"You do realize I was just about to leave for my lunch break?" Alex said once she answered the phone.

Hawk chuckled. "I purposely waited to call you. Better to get you now than in the morning *before* you've pumped coffee into your veins."

"Perhaps—but I'll only be slightly more pleasant now. Keeping me from my lunch is a move that might backfire on you."

Hawk turned on his headlights and eased onto the gas. "Well, I won't keep you long. I just wanted to let you know I've arrived and am on my way to the destination."

"Excellent. I'll make a note of your progress." She paused for a moment. "As a matter of fact, I think I have you on our satellite feed. Are you driving a light-colored Toyota Forerunner?"

"That'd be me, though so is the rest of the country."

"Unless the rest of the country has already been tagged with GPS tracking devices that match your identifier, I think it's a safe bet I'm looking at you."

"Excellent. You can watch me screw everything up on a slight eight-second delay."

"That's hardly a delay at all."

"Long enough to win a bull riding competition."

"Well, at least I'll know where to send the team to retrieve your dead body once you fall off a bull."

"Actually, I called for another reason."

"Oh?"

"Yeah, I heard you got caught trying to sneak into The Vault at CIA headquarters."

"Who told you that?"

"Blunt, but that's not important. What *is* important is why you did it—and please tell me you didn't do it for me."

"So you're okay with me lying to you?"

"Come on, Alex. This isn't funny. I appreciate everything you're doing for me regarding my father, but I don't want this to be something that jeopardizes your own future. It's not worth it. I've survived this long without knowing all the intimate details about who he is; I'm sure a few more years won't be the death of me. However, it might be the death of *your* career."

"If it makes you feel any better, I didn't find much on your father."

"Actually, that makes me feel worse." He paused. "Did you find *anything*?"

"An empty folder with Franklin Foster's name on the tab. For whatever reason, someone at the CIA thought it best to remove the files altogether. The folder is likely the only trace of him ever existing at the agency."

"Did they know what you were after?"

"I doubt it. Believe it or not, The Vault is one of the few places that doesn't have surveillance cameras inside. They had to play their hunches because I didn't tell them anything."

"How'd you get out?"

"It always helps to have leverage on the Director."

"You have dirt on Coker?"

"Something like that."

Hawk laughed. "You've got guts, Alex. I'll give that to you."

"Without them, I'd be nowhere in this business."

"I hope they serve us well on this mission."

"They will." She sighed. "But I didn't leave head-quarters empty handed."

"Did you use the magic trick I taught you?"

"Actually, it came in handy in acquiring a cell phone after they caught me."

"This I've got to hear."

"I'd love to talk more, but I've got a meeting with General Johnson in ten minutes that I need to prepare for."

"Okay, fine. Leave me hanging."

"I will forward you the entire itinerary for your trip so if you go dark, you have everything you need and won't have to compromise your mission."

"Roger that."

"But Hawk," she said, "I do have something we need to talk about."

"I'm listening."

"No, this isn't the kind of thing we need to talk about over the phone. We'll talk about it when you get back."

"So, you're giving me something to live for? Trying to make sure I don't act foolishly during this mission?"

"You can take it however you like. But you're gonna want to hear it."

"Don't worry—I'm already looking forward to it."

Hawk hung up and stared up through his windshield at the first stars of the evening twinkling on the horizon. He needed to stay focused on the mission, but he couldn't help but wonder what Alex had learned.

CHAPTER 10

MUSA DEMBY PEERED through his scope at the target set up two hundred meters away. He always thought it was ridiculous that anyone ever shot at a piece of paper with a circular target highlighted with a bullseye. "There's no single point that's a bullseye," he often said, scoffing at his aides. "Bullseye is when you hit your target—and he dies."

He steadied his hand and his breathing. The target he saw through his scope was that of an armed dummy perched in a tree. His spotter would confirm if he hit it or not.

Slowly, Demby squeezed the trigger—*crack*! He'd barely moved, keeping his eye trained on his mark. He didn't need his lackey to tell him if he hit the target after he watched the dummy tumble to the ground.

"Direct hit!" Demby's lackey said as he jumped into the air. "Excellent shooting!"

Demby slapped the aide in the side of the head. "Even a water buffalo in Kenya could've seen the target fall out of the tree."

"Sorry, sir," the lackey said.

"Go set him back up," Demby said in his choppy English accent. "You've got five minutes before I start shooting again."

The lackey raced toward the tree, grabbed the dummy target, and reset it. But Demby didn't wait five minutes. He barely waited three before he fired again, hitting the target in the head and sending it back toward the ground. The aide pivoted and rushed back toward the it—but he didn't get far.

Demby snickered as he squeezed off another shot, this one exploding in the back of the lackey's head. He turned toward the rest of the handful of men who'd joined him. "So, who wants to replace the target now?"

No one budged.

A grin spread across Demby's face. "No worries. I can barely see anything now anyway. Let's call it a day." He rubbed the head of a young boy toting a rifle next to him. "What do you say?"

The boy, who barely looked a day over ten years old, looked up at Demby and flashed a faint smile.

Demby slung his rifle over his shoulder and marched toward the three vehicles waiting near the road just off the small clearing. The drive back to Koidu wouldn't take long, and it'd give him time to contemplate how he was going to deal with the most challenging problem he'd faced in a while: getting his product to clients.

From every visible standard, Demby ran a legitimate diamond export corporation. Sefadu Holdings, located in Koidu, was founded when many of the multinational mining operations pulled out, leaving several mines abandoned overnight. The companies cited reasons for their sudden departure: civil unrest, Ebola outbreak, and inability to recruit competent staff to Sierra Leone. But all the locals knew the truth: The mines had been stripped. With nothing much of value remaining, the companies didn't want to continue hemorrhaging money.

But Demby was managing one of mines for a Belgian firm and lied to management about the lack of diamonds in one of the open-pits he oversaw. He'd begun pocketing some of the diamonds and had amassed a healthy bank account in the process. Desperate to get a higher yield, the company used block caving to extend the life of their surface mines by sending them underground. However, it wasn't enough to sustain operations. When the firm decided to pull out, Demby made them a paltry offer for the land rights and equipment, but it was far more than they could earn if they dismantled everything and returned it to Belgium. So they agreed to his proposal and Sefadu Holdings began operations.

Demby was careful not to announce an ore discovery too soon. And when he did, he made sure it sounded modest. His shrewd business dealings ensured that he didn't bring scrutiny on himself from his former employers *and* that he could quietly create a black market on the side that might be far more profitable. To industry observers, Sefadu Holdings looked like a struggling mining operation. Meanwhile, Demby was cashing in on his calculated efforts to create a small empire. In less than two years, he'd gone from being an underpaid employee to the *de facto* King of Koidu.

When Demby and his convoy arrived at The Errant Apostrophe's, a bar run by an aspiring British writer, they crammed into their usual booth in the back. A thatched roof was all that separated patrons from the natural surroundings as the pub was built in the foothills of the Tingi Mountains.

Demby spoke in English with a thick African accent, splicing in a few words in Krio whenever he couldn't find the word he wanted. He ordered a shot for all his cohorts and proposed a toast.

"To the good life," he roared.

The men clinked their glasses together and downed the liquor. Demby motioned for the bartender to come over and deliver another round for everyone. After two more shots, he was ready to start talking.

"Gentlemen, we have a serious problem," he said as he leaned forward on the table, his arms crossed. "And I need your advice on what we should do about it."

One of his most trusted aides, Ibrahim, eyed his boss closely. "What kind of problem?"

Demby stroked his thin beard. "Government interference is making it more difficult for us to get our diamonds to Al Hasib."

"We can't transport them using airlines?" one of the other aides asked.

Demby shook his head. "It's getting too expensive. Someone else has taken over the customs department and has raised our price. Unfortunately, it's a price we can't afford to pay. So, we must seek an alternative."

"What about a run to Liberia?"

Demby shrugged. "That's a last resort. It's still expensive to pay the border agents there, plus there's the added expense of employing more people, which means less profit for everyone."

"We certainly don't want that," Ibrahim said.

"Exactly. We must consider other alternatives."

Ibrahim stared out into the distance for a moment before responding. "What about your humanitarian agency?"

Demby's shrewd skills as a businessman extended far beyond swindling and lying to his former employer. When an opportunity arose, he sought an easy solution, choosing to grease palms rather than exchange punches. He also surmised that convincing locals that he had their best interest at heart through his investments was better than trying to plead with them. This epiphany led to the development of SLAM, Sierra Leone Aid & Medical Supply Company. He admitted it could've had a better name, but it was effective enough with the locals, especially when the clinics started cropping up all across the eastern region of the country.

He hired an American doctor, Alissa Ackerman, to run SLAM and wasn't disappointed. In just under two years, she'd managed to make the organization a household name with locals for all the services it provided. People living in the bush would walk three days through the jungle to a clinic if they got injured during a hunt. Women who normally would've lost their babies during pregnancy were now being monitored more closely, resulting in a much lower mortality rate for both mothers and babies. Ebola education spread rapidly throughout the eastern region of the country, resulting in the decline of Ebola deaths. And it was all due to her efforts.

"Alissa wouldn't let me risk SLAM's reputation on

an endeavor like this," Demby said before he tossed back another shot.

"Since when did you ever ask for permission?" Ibrahim asked.

A smile spread across Demby's face as he slapped Ibrahim on the back. "You've got a point." He paused. "But she must never know. If she ever finds out, I'm blaming all of you."

"If I ever find out what?" came a woman's voice from behind Demby.

He looked over his shoulder, and his eyebrows shot upward as he realized Alissa had made it to the bar. "If you ever find out how much I care about you."

"You? Care about someone?" she scoffed. "I'll believe it when I see it."

Realizing he'd avoided revealing the true nature of their conversation, he smiled at her. "I do care about people," Demby said. "I know it may be difficult for you to believe, but it's true."

She sat down at the table across from Demby and ordered a drink. "The only thing that's difficult for me to believe is that you have a heart." She paused and slowly shook her head, never taking her gaze off Demby. "Even when I press my stethoscope against your chest, I still have a hard time believing that anything beats inside of there."

He stared at her. The feisty American brunette always managed to rile him up. He'd only made one advance on her and was summarily rejected. But he figured that she'd eventually succumb to his charm.

Demby looked at Ibrahim, who stared at her, mouth agape.

"She just insulted you," Ibrahim said.

Her jabs didn't bother Demby. "She can insult me all she wants. I just want her."

"The one woman you can't have," Ibrahim quipped.

"One day, my friend, one day."

She threw back another shot and stared at Demby. "I know you're lying." She took a deep breath. "What were you really talking about?"

"The weather," Demby said. "We were talking about the weather."

In the background, some reggae beats pumped from the jukebox.

She laughed. "You're a terrible liar. How you ever gained so much power in this city is a mystery to me."

Demby paused and decided to tell her the truth—in a light-hearted way. He was betting that she wouldn't believe him. "If you must know, I told them that we were going to smuggle diamonds out of the country to terrorists using SLAM." He froze and watched for her reaction.

She broke into laughter. "You really are insane.

Maybe next time I'll inspect your brain."

"It's all there," he said. "Skull and all."

"It's not the skull that I'm worried about. It's what's inside the skull that frightens me; there's a distinct possibility that there isn't much left inside there," she quipped as she pointed at his head.

"I promise you, there's more there than you can handle."

She flashed a wry grin. "If you insist."

"Oh, I do," Demby said. "In fact, I'll prove it to you."

She winked at him. "What? By killing a few brain cells?"

One of Demby's assistants dropped a glass bottle of rum on the table. "Let the brain cell killing begin."

Demby snatched the bottle up and filled both his glass and Alissa's. "I hope you like the taste of defeat."

She threw her head back and laughed. "I hope you like the taste of rum," she said, raising her glass. "That is, if you think you can keep up with me."

They both tossed back their shots and slammed their glasses on the table.

"Tomorrow's going to be a rough day for you, Doctor Ackerman," Demby said as he poured the pair another drink. "That much I can promise you."

"Bring it on," she said.

Ibrahim nudged his boss and spoke softly, "Much

more of this and she won't remember her name, let alone what you might be slipping into her trucks."

Demby winked at Ibrahim and raised his glass in the air, smiling as he stared across the table at her. "Ibrahim, have I told you lately that you're smarter than you look?"

Ibrahim beamed as he shook his head.

"Well, you are," Demby said as he tossed back another drink. He leaned in close to Ibrahim. "You're in charge of sneaking the product out using the SLAM aid trucks." He grabbed the front of Ibrahim's shirt. "Don't disappoint me. I'd hate to have to hurt her."

Ibrahim nodded knowingly. "You have nothing to worry about."

CHAPTER 11

WHEN IT CAME TO MANAGING FIRESTORM, Blunt preferred to simplify the operations. Hawk served as primary problem solver for most missions, while two other operatives worked on ancillary projects—Hal Beckham and Bo Lowman. Collectively, Blunt called the trio, "The Killer B's", his own tip of the cap to the nickname given to a handful of long-since retired sluggers from the Houston Astros. However, he assigned them code names, aside from Hawk, who he decided giving a code name to would be a shame when his given name was sufficient. Beckham went by Thor, and Lowman went by Zeus. Hawk's seldomly used code name was Ares. Blunt conceded that the names weren't creative, but he was aiming for practicality, not originality. Two Greek gods and a Norse one—all mythological names for an agency that he preferred to remain a myth in spy circles.

Blunt used Hawk on every mission when he was available. If a new mission came in and it could wait,

Blunt would wait until Hawk returned. But this time, it couldn't. Hawk's assignment in Sierra Leone was of utmost importance, both to putting a major dent in Al Hasib's operations as well as for recovering the stolen weapons from Colton Industries. And pulling him out suddenly might risk tipping off Musa Demby that someone was on to him. Blunt resigned himself to the fact that he'd have to use his second best option: Thor.

Thor was forced out of MI6 after going rogue on several missions, a fact that didn't bother Blunt. When assessing whether an operative was the right fit, Blunt only looked at the results—and Thor's results sparkled. Working under deep cover, Thor once goaded two weapons dealers into a showdown. The result was the largest recovery of black market weapons in the history of MI6. And while Thor didn't have to fire a single shot, he was chastised for kidnapping the Prince of Monaco to incite the conflict. Repercussions aside, Thor more than impressed Blunt.

With Hawk gone on assignment, Blunt needed to move quickly to get Thor engaged. Blunt followed contact protocol by placing an ad in *The New York Times*, an archaic way of communicating in the 21st Century but still effective when it came to spy craft. Two days later, Blunt was standing in front of a painting in the Byzantine collection inside the National

Gallery of Art at precisely 11:00 a.m. when Thor approached. Blunt stood about six feet away and stared at the piece of art before uttering a word.

"This is a fine painting," Thor said.

"Yes, it is," Blunt replied. "Almost as fine as the art in the second stall of the men's bathroom."

And with that, Blunt's work was finished. All the details of Thor's assignment had been burned onto a flash drive from a laptop computer that had never been connected to the Internet. Leery of digital signatures, Blunt exercised the utmost caution when working on such sensitive missions.

The instructions for Thor were simple: a date, a location, a time, and a target. The method was also strongly suggested: Make it look like an accident.

Blunt could only imagine what Thor would think when he saw the name of the man he was to eliminate: Liam Jepsen, the prime minister of Denmark.

CHAPTER 12

THE FAINT OUTLINE of the sunbaked letters on the Jourbert Safaris wooden sign saved Hawk from spending the night in his Forerunner. As he pulled through the gate and surveyed the property, he wondered if the untended grounds were a result of the operation recently re-opening for business after a long hiatus or the general inattention to upkeep that seemed germane to the entire continent. Were it not for the light emanating from a window at the corner of a building, he would've assumed the place was abandoned.

After he parked, Hawk grabbed his gear and marched toward the entrance, one that was demarcated with a hand-drawn sign on a piece of paper. A screen door was shut, but the main door was wide open. Hawk eased into the lobby area, which was illuminated only by a faint amount of light coming from the bottom of a door behind the counter.

"Hello?" he called in his Kiwi accent. "Anybody here?"

Hawk scanned the room. It was tight, furnished with two folding chairs and a coffee table covered in hunting magazines. A clock hung on the wall behind the counter and ticked with the passing of each second.

"Hello?"

After a few moments, the door behind the counter swung open and a small Asian man shuffled out into the lobby and flicked the light switch. Nothing happened.

"Oh, the damn power is out again," muttered the man. "Welcome to Sierra Leone."

Hawk chuckled. "Sierra Leone doesn't have the corner on the market for power outages in Africa. It's an epidemic."

"More prevalent than Ebola?" the man shot back.

Hawk couldn't tell if he was joking or not but concluded nervous laughter was better than no laughter at all.

"It's a joke," the man said as he squinted at the paper. "Be right back." Less than a half minute later, he returned carrying a candle, the one that had been providing the light in his office. "Now, let's see here. You must be Oliver Martin."

Hawk nodded.

"And you're from New Zealand?"

"Yes, the mystical land of adventure and hobbits."

The man stopped and looked up from his paperwork. "Hobbits?"

"Never mind. It's from a movie."

"Ah, movies," the man said. "We don't get to watch many of those—or at least finish them. Never know when you're suddenly going to be sitting in the dark."

Hawk smiled. "That's a good metaphor for life."

The man eyed Hawk closely. "You obviously haven't been to Sierra Leone before. No one who lived here would say that."

"What would someone from Sierra Leone say about life?"

"They'd say, 'You're alive. Good. Now just try not to die today.'"

"An even better metaphor for life—well, at least the people around me."

The man scribbled on the paper and asked Hawk for his signature. "My name is Joon Yun, and I manage the lodging here. If you have any questions, you can knock on this door at any time, and I'll be happy to help you."

"What time does my hunting party leave in the morning?" Hawk asked.

Yun laughed. "Party? You mean *you* and your guide?" He didn't wait for an answer. "Breakfast is served at five-thirty down the hall, and you will leave at six for the hunt." He slid a key and an information sheet across the counter to Hawk. "Your room is the first one on the left down the hall. Enjoy your stay."

Hawk started down the hallway before he stopped and turned around. "You know where I can get a cold drink and some food around here at this time of night?"

Yun glanced at the clock on the wall behind. "There's a bar about a mile down the road on the left. They will have something for you."

Hawk found his room, threw his equipment inside, and locked the door. He couldn't ignore his stomach's rumblings any longer.

Five minutes later, he strode into The Errant Apostrophe's and sat down at a table in a vacant corner of the room. His intent was to drink a beer, eat some meat, and retire for the evening. But a poker game broke out.

Minutes after he ordered his food, a trio of men sat down at the table next to him. One of the men Hawk thought looked like an illegal arms dealer from South Africa from a photo he'd seen once in a CIA report. Hawk couldn't be sure. But whoever the man was, Hawk sensed trouble.

The man cut his eyes over at Hawk and pulled out a deck of cards. "You play poker?"

Hawk glanced at him and pointed at his own chest. "Me?"

"Well, I ain't talking about the oke sitting behind you," the man said in a thick South African accent.

Hawk shrugged. "I play from time to time."

"Pull up a chair. I'll deal you in. It'll be a jol."

Hawk joined the men. "Oliver Martin."

"What are you? A fashion designer?" the man groused. His companions both chuckled.

"I'm in taxidermy. Here on a hunting expedition."

"Well, Oliver Martin, with a name like that, I think you chose the wrong profession."

Hawk pounced on the opportunity to plant a seed that might come to fruition sooner rather than later. "Only if you don't need to get your kills out of the country. I have quite the export license."

"Expecting to kill something you're going to need to export?"

Hawk nodded.

He looked Hawk up and down before smiling. "I doubt you'll need any such license for your trip here this time, mate." The man winked. "My name is Keanu Visser, and these two okes are forgettable, so you don't need to worry with their names."

One of the other men lit a cigar and blew a ring of smoke. He then glared at Visser. "I'm Soto—and you'll remember me because I'm the one who's going to take all your money."

"We'll see about that," chimed in the remaining

nameless man. "I'm Perryman, and both of these blokes are full of it, mate. *I'm* the one who's going to take all your money."

An hour later, Hawk raked the remaining pot in front of him and declared himself the winner.

"You need to come back tomorrow and give me a chance to win my money back," Visser said before chugging the rest of his beer.

Hawk stood up. "No promises. I've got a hunt in the morning, but I'll see what I can do."

***

THE NEXT MORNING came early for Hawk. He groaned as he rolled out of bed and quickly dressed himself. Breakfast consisted of oatmeal and a banana. When he finished, his guide met him on the front steps of the outfitter's main building.

"Ethan Jacobs," said the guide. "Are you ready for a fun day of hunting with this motley crew?" He gestured toward his Range Rover.

Hawk noticed several familiar faces packed into the vehicle. All three of the men he played poker with waved at him.

"Let's go, Martin," Visser said. "I hate losing, and I need to win my money back."

Hawk sauntered over to the Range Rover. "What

makes you think you're going to win it back?"

"What makes you think I won't?" Visser snapped. "How about double or nothing on our hunt today? Whoever kills an animal with the farthest shot wins."

Hawk put on a concerned look and hesitated.

Visser goaded him on. "What's the matter, mate? You scared you might lose?"

After another moment of silence, Hawk finally responded to the request. "Since you insist—"

"Good. Now that that's settled, shall we be on our way?" Jacobs said as he climbed into the driver's seat and cranked the engine.

Hawk opened the door to the backseat and gestured for Perryman to move to the center so he could sit on the side.

Perryman's eyes narrowed. "You can sit in the middle."

"Is that any way to treat your poker champion? Besides, I get motion sickness rather easily."

They drove an hour south until they turned off the main road and bumped along a dirt road that had appeared as if it wasn't properly maintained. Potholes the size of small children and small bodies of water stretched across the road made for an interesting next five miles.

Once Jacobs parked the vehicle, they piled out. "I hope you gentlemen are ready. This is going to be some of the best duiker hunting you've ever experienced in your entire lives."

They drew lots to see who would shoot first. That honor fell to Visser. Hawk was second.

Two hours into their hunt, they came across a duiker foraging near a stream. Visser took aim and dropped the animal on his first shot from about seventy-five meters.

Thirty minutes later, it was Hawk's turn. His shot, however, was from a much farther distance. Jacobs estimated it to be no less than 200 meters.

Hawk pulled the trigger, and a bullet ripped down the hillside. The duiker crashed to the ground as if it had been instantly put to sleep. Hawk patted Visser on the back. "That's how you do it."

Jacobs hustled toward the animal, followed by Soto and Perryman. Hawk moved to fall in line, but Visser grabbed him by back of shirt and yanked him backward.

"What's this all about?" Hawk asked.

Visser grabbed Hawk's arm and twisted it before he jammed a gun beneath Hawk's chin. "That's funny. I was just about to ask you the same thing. Now, who are you, Oliver Martin?"

CHAPTER 13

THE HUM OF LARGE EQUIPMENT rumbling across the grounds of Sefadu Holdings' mine sounded like music to the ears of Musa Demby. Given the opportunity to blossom, Demby's entrepreneurial skills were finally producing what he always dreamed possible: truckloads of money. The diamond firms in Antwerp were calling him daily, resulting in a steady profit flow. But the amount the Belgian companies paid him for his raw diamonds paled in comparison to what Al Hasib forked over for rocks the terrorist group would eventually place on the black market. Demby believed in diversification, but he favored the highest bidder.

By the time Demby arrived on site, the grounds were like a hive of activity. Large trucks were carting out processed soil. Excavators scraped away at the soil. Workers sifted through the dirt in the open-pit mine. Engineers plotted their next blast in order to convert portions of the mine into the underground variety.

Joined by Ibrahim, Demby followed the circular route to the bottom of one of the open-pit mines. He kicked at the dirt as he listened to a synopsis report from his top aide.

"Did you make contact yet with Al Hasib?" Demby asked.

Ibrahim nodded. "They said they are willing to wait up to a week longer if that's what it takes to ensure they get the diamonds without incident. The last thing they want is anyone figuring out what they're doing."

"And that's the last thing we want too." Demby stopped and scanned the grounds. "If we can maintain a portion of our operations as compliant with regulations and continue to exist as a reputable firm, no one will ever take this away from us. No matter what we do, we must be careful."

"I understand."

Demby put his hands on his hips and eyed Ibrahim closely. "So, do you think we can use SLAM to transport the diamonds to Al Hasib?"

Ibrahim shrugged. "At this point, I'm not sure. We still have some more work to do."

"The most important thing is that Alissa doesn't find out. She could ruin everything if she knew what we were doing."

"Agreed. I'll make sure she never suspects anything."

Demby slapped Ibrahim on the back. "Excellent. I expect nothing less."

They both continued to amble down the road. After another fifty meters of walking in silence, an explosion shook the earth. Instinctively, both men dove to the ground as they watched a plume of smoke and dust encompass the area.

"I hope that's part of the block caving process," Demby said as he glanced at Ibrahim.

Ibrahim shook his head. "I'm afraid it's not."

After the dust cleared, Demby heard frantic shouting coming from the mine below, followed by screaming. He stood up and brushed himself off before looking at ground zero of the explosion.

"It seems like we have a problem on our hands," Ibrahim said.

Demby scowled. "A problem?"

"The mine just collapsed."

"Are you sure?"

"I'd bet my life on it."

Demby broke into a sprint down the road. "Then we don't have much time to lose. We can't let all those good diamonds go to waste."

Ibrahim shouted after his boss, hustling to keep pace. "There are workers trapped inside."

"Workers can be replaced."

Ibrahim frowned. "Everyone's going to know

something happened."

"We've been blasting in these mines for how many years now? Nobody will suspect a thing."

"Maybe not now, but eventually they will when these men don't return home to their families."

"You leave that to me. We can't experience any more delays in getting these diamonds to Al Hasib. You know what they'll do to us. Their favor toward us will only last so long."

After they arrived at the entrance to the mine, they surveyed the damage. The opening was covered by rock and other debris. Workers shoveled away the pieces blocking their way. One of the foremen shouted directions while his subordinates carried out the orders.

Demby saw a man's hand sticking out of the rock. As he got closer, he could hear the man pleading for help.

"I'm right here. Can anyone help me get free?" the worker said.

Demby knelt down. "I can."

"Oh, thank you."

"There's just one thing I need you to do for me first."

"I swear I can't do anything right now. I can barely move. I can't even feel my legs."

"Just hand me what you collected today."

The man's hand disappeared beneath the rubble only to emerge again a few seconds later clutching a pouch of diamonds. Demby tugged it from the man's hand.

"Very well then," Demby said. He proceeded to shovel dirt and more debris onto the opening.

The worker panicked. "You said you'd help me. Come on."

Demby continued to rake more dirt on the opening above the man until his voice was muffled to almost a whisper beneath the weight of the rubble. He then stood up and dusted off his hands.

Searching for a high point in the mine, he found an excavator and climbed on top of the cab. "Gentlemen, it's time to go home. Go ahead and take the rest of the day off. We'll double our efforts in different mines tomorrow. There's nothing more we can do to help."

A few of the men started shouting back at Demby.

"We can't just leave them," one of the men said. "They're going to die if we don't help them."

"They're going to die even if you do. They're as good as dead."

The man scowled. "I can't stand by and do nothing." He bent over and started shoveling rocks to the side.

Demby yanked out his pistol and shot the man in

the head then hopped down from the cab. "Anyone else care to disagree?"

Nobody said a word. A few shook their head.

"Good. I'm glad we're all in agreement."

Ibrahim rushed up to him. "Do you think these men are seriously going to leave their friends to die in the mine like this?"

"I'm counting on it."

"And what makes you think they're going to go along with it?"

"Because everyone likes getting paid—and nobody else wants to die."

Demby grinned as he watched the workers begin to climb out of the mine and head home for the day.

CHAPTER 14

FOR A MAN WHO PREFERRED to work in the shadows, Blunt spent plenty of time in the daylight, soaking up the sun whenever he had an opportunity. Surviving D.C. winters was something that made him pine for the Texas sunshine. So when he had any free time during his workday, Blunt walked around the National Mall. He claimed it helped him clear his mind. But the truth is the sunshine served as his antidote to depression.

During these walks, he was often acknowledged by other Capitol Hill employees, some staffers and some politicians. But it was never more than a slight head nod or a touch to the brim of man's fedora.

Until today.

As Blunt was circling the National Mall for the second time that morning, he almost stumbled to the ground as a man bumped into him from behind.

"Hey, watch what you're—" Blunt froze for a moment then scanned the area. "What are you doing here?" he asked in a loud whisper.

"Don't worry," the man said. "I wasn't followed."

"I should hope not, but that doesn't change the fact that this breaks protocol. I'm never to be approached in public or contacted in the open. You ought to know that by now."

The man nodded knowingly. "I understand, but this just couldn't wait."

"What couldn't wait?"

"What I'm about to tell you and show you."

Blunt's eyes widened. "Are you out of your freakin' mind? You're jeopardizing everything just by being here."

"I'm afraid we're past that point."

"What do you mean?"

The man handed Blunt a manila folder. "Take a look at these."

"Where'd you get these?" Blunt demanded.

"It doesn't matter. What does matter is that someone is on to you; someone is on to Firestorm. And they're going to shut down the organization as soon as possible if you don't do something."

"Who's *they*?"

"There's another shadow organization, ironically named Searchlight. They're completely independent of any government entity, fully funded through private means. The rumor is that they're making a play to move to the top of the food chain."

"Who's behind all this?" Blunt asked as he continued to study the report in his hands along with several photos.

"It's best that I don't tell you the *who*. But I can take care of the *who* for you."

Blunt shrugged. "Then by all means, don't waste any time."

The man looked around nervously as he led Blunt off the main path and to a nearby patch of bushes. Putting his arm around Blunt, the man said, "I'm going to need some more assurances. I'm sure you understand."

"Such as?"

"Twenty percent more to take care of him."

"Twenty percent more? Are you nuts?"

"Take it or leave it."

Blunt sighed and stared at the glimmering water. "Fine. Twenty percent it is."

"Great. Just wire me the money. Once I see it in my account, I'll take care of the problem."

"It'll be there," Blunt said. "Now, get outta here."

The man collected the folder back from Blunt. "I'll only need forty-eight hours."

Blunt watched the man scurry away into a shady patch of trees nearby. He hadn't gone more than fifty meters until he collapsed to the ground.

Blunt rushed over to him. "Talk to me. Are you okay?"

No response.

Blunt called 9-1-1 and reported their location to the dispatcher.

"Don't die on me yet," Blunt said as he studied the man's face. "The paramedics are already on their way."

"Run," the man said. "Get out of the shadows or you might be next."

Blunt didn't know if the man was speaking figuratively or literally, but he didn't want to stick around to find out. He grabbed the folder and cell phone from the man and scampered toward the main sidewalk into the open.

Who the hell is behind Searchlight?

CHAPTER 15

HAWK REMAINED CONSTRICTED by Visser's grip and somewhat concerned about the gun shoved underneath his chin. Struggling to break free, Hawk decided to relax for a moment and opt for a different way out of the situation.

"What do you want?" he asked.

"I think I've already made it clear what I want," Visser said. "I want to know who you are."

"I already told you: I'm Oliver Martin."

"And I'm supposed to believe that load of rubbish?"

"It's true. I swear. I've got no reason to pretend to be someone else."

Visser tightened his grip. "That remains to be seen. Now, who are you really?"

"I already told you. I'm an exporter from New Zealand."

"You sure about that?"

"Look me up. I have a website. Martin Exports.com. My firm deals in all types of antiquities and rare items that must be transported between countries. Air, sea, land—it doesn't matter. We do it all."

Visser relaxed and released Hawk. "If I find out you've been lying to me—"

Hawk did his best to act scared, putting up his hands in surrender as Visser kept his gun trained on him. "I haven't. I promise. I might even be able to help you if you have something that needs to be moved. I'm not here to judge, but perhaps you do."

"What's that supposed to mean?"

"Nothing. Nothing. Just if you need help, I can help you."

"You have a license that can get dead exotic animals out of one country and into another?"

Hawk winked—and continued trolling the waters to see if Visser was more than he let on. "Dead animals are easier to move than you might think. And sometimes they can help you get other things out of the country."

"Such as?"

"You name it, though I won't because I never ask my clients about such matters. Quite frankly, it's none of my business."

Visser eyed Hawk closely. "But that shot back there—that wasn't just some ordinary shot, was it?"

Their guide had realized he'd lost two members of his party and tramped back through the thick brush to find them. "What are you two doing back here?" Jacobs asked. "The others are up ahead—and we've spotted a bongo."

"A bongo?" Visser asked. "Here?"

"They're not as rare as you might think," Jacobs said. "Now if you want to see one, grab your guns and get moving."

After they joined the rest of their party and traipsed along through the jungle for a few moments, Jacobs held up his hand.

"The bongo is just up ahead on the right," Jacobs said peering through his binoculars. "Does everyone see it?"

All the hunters put their binoculars to their eyes and strained to see the large beast in the distance.

"This would complete our day," Jacobs said. "Anyone want to take the first shot?"

"I will," Visser volunteered.

"Be my guest," Jacobs said, gesturing in the direction of the large animals.

Visser knelt down and positioned his gun on a nearby fallen tree. Hawk joined.

"What are you doing?" Visser asked. "I said I'd take the first shot."

"And I'm here for when you miss," Hawk quipped, followed by a wink.

Visser steadied his gun on the log and waited for a moment. He exhaled and waited some more before he finally squeezed the trigger. The bullet whizzed through the thick brush, disrupting the otherwise calm jungle.

He missed.

The bongo lifted its head in panic before bounding away.

It didn't get more than another ten meters before Hawk unleashed a shot that dropped the animal almost immediately.

Jacobs excitedly grabbed Hawk's tricep and gave it a squeeze. "Did you see that? What did you say you did again?"

Hawk stared out at his kill. "I deal in exports."

"Well, that's one helluva shot, Mr. Export Man. I don't know many people who can do that."

"Got lucky, I guess."

Visser ripped his sunglasses off and glared at Hawk. "Lucky, my ass. That's a sniper-level shot right there."

Hawk shrugged. "I spend a lot of time practicing at the range."

"Who doesn't?"

Jacobs started to chuckle. "Apparently you need to spend more time there." He motioned for everyone to follow him. "Let's go look at Mr. Martin's kill."

Visser grabbed Hawk by the arm, impeding him from joining Jacobs. "Exports, you say?"

Hawk stopped and nodded. "Do you need something?"

Visser looked Hawk up and down. "We need to talk."

CHAPTER 16

AS DUSK FELL, MUSA DEMBY gathered with some of his men at the mine office. Several foremen who'd escaped the collapse informed Demby they'd received phone calls from anxious girlfriends, wives, and mothers, all wondering where their men were. They were running out of stories to tell.

"I'm sure someone will help us," one of the foremen said. "This isn't the first time a mine has collapsed. They even made a movie about the men who rescued the miners in Chile."

"They're not going to make a movie about anything that happens in Sierra Leone, much less come help us," Demby said. "We have to settle this our way."

Another man with a furrowed brow stepped forward. "So, what is *our* way? To let them die beneath the rubble? Is that any way for us to act?"

Demby's narrowed his eyes. "We don't have the resources or the time to save them. And if we're all honest with ourselves, we know they'll all be dead before we can get to them."

"Maybe not all of them," said another foreman, Akili. "I was down there a half hour ago. There were some men who were just beneath the surface. It wouldn't take much to rescue them."

Demby paced around the room before he stopped dramatically, stomping his foot when he did. He fixed his gaze on Akili. "And who would rescue these men?"

Akili shrugged. "I don't know. Us? Other workers along with people in the city? Everyone would be willing to help, I'm sure."

"I don't have time for this," Demby said with a sneer. "Any rescue mission is going to cost this mine more than two million dollars due to the lost time. We have a deadline to make, and my clients won't tolerate any delays."

"These men are being suffocated and crushed beneath the weight of the debris," Akili argued. "We can't just stand by and let that happen."

"We can and we will. Besides, that's nothing compared to what my client might do to all of us if we miss the delivery deadline." Demby circled the room once again. "Now, let's give these men who are trapped a merciful ending. Round up the rest of our demolition team and put them to work. I want that area demolished as soon as possible with no trace of what happened. Is that understood?"

Almost every man nodded—everyone except Akili, that is.

"No. You can't let those men die like this. I won't let you do it," Akili protested.

Demby unholstered his pistol and wheeled in Akili's direction. Demby stopped and trained his gun on his contentious subordinate.

"Then you can join them," Demby said.

Akili put his hands up in surrender. "Okay, okay. You've made your point."

"Does anyone else want to protest?" Demby said as he turned to face the rest of the men.

He waited briefly as the room remained silent.

"Very well then. Now, go round up the demolition team."

CHAPTER 17

ALEX DUNCAN STOPPED HER MIDDAY RUN short when her phone started buzzing again. She'd sent the first call straight to voicemail with the click of a button without even bothering to see who it was. Her regular exercise routine calmed and centered her like nothing else could—not even yoga. Her time wasn't to be interrupted. But today, it couldn't be helped.

When the phone vibrated again with another call immediately after she'd ignored the first one, she knew it could only be one person.

"Senator, sorry. I was running," she said as she tried to catch her breath. "What's so urgent?"

"I need you to look into something for me right away," Blunt said.

"What's going on?"

He exhaled. "I'm not sure. But this morning around ten o'clock, I was approached by a man who told me about another shadow organization called Searchlight."

117

"Never heard of it."

"Me neither, which really made me question if it exists. But I implicitly trust the source, and he told me that Searchlight was making a play to shut down Firestorm."

"And how would they do that?"

"I'm not sure, but my source died moments after he told me this."

"You saw him die?"

"Yeah. I was at the National Mall when he surprised me with a visit and then collapsed right after he finished meeting with me."

"Who is this source?"

"Plausible deniability, Alex," he grunted. "There are some things it's best you don't know—and it's for your own good."

"So, you want me to look into Searchlight?"

"Would you? And do it right away?"

"I'll do my best. I'm also working with Hawk right now, remember?"

"Have you heard from him lately?"

"He's fine. He made it to Sierra Leone and made contact with the outfitter he was scheduled to meet."

"Anything else?"

"Not yet, but I'm keeping an eye on the mine. They had some kind of explosion there, but I haven't been able to find out anything through the news."

"Keep me posted, and find out what you can as soon as possible on Searchlight. I want to know who we need to put in the crosshairs."

Alex hung up and finished her run, her mind spinning with possibilities over the turf war about to take place between two black ops programs. She felt confident that Hawk gave Firestorm the upper hand.

***

FRESHLY SHOWERED, ALEX WALKED back into the office with a new sense of urgency and purpose. She sat down at her desk and concluded that before she continued with her task, she needed a power ballad.

Adele should do the trick.

Her favorite Adele album began pumping through her computer speakers as she started pounding on the keyboard in search of answers.

Searchlight, who are you?

For the next hour, her searches led her from one dead end to the next. She decided to phone her friend at the CIA, Mallory Kauffman, and find out if she'd heard anything.

"Searchlight?" Mallory asked. "That name doesn't ring a bell, but that doesn't mean much."

"It'd sure mean a lot to me if you could figure out

who's behind it."

"I'll do some poking around, but if you can't find anything, I doubt I'll be able to. You're the one with all the freedom out there to hack away until your heart's content, free from all repercussions."

"That doesn't work so well when you don't have a starting point. I literally know nothing other than what Blunt told me."

"Which was what?"

"That they're trying to take down Firestorm, and the man who told Blunt about it today was assassinated at the National Mall."

"Assassinated? Like gunned down?"

"Blunt didn't get into specifics, but he did say the man collapsed."

"Find me a name. I'm sure there might be a medical report somewhere or a responding unit that details who paramedics attended to. I mean, I'm assuming he isn't still just lying there dead."

"I doubt the guy gave anyone his name, especially if died per Blunt's report about the incident."

Mallory sighed. "Aliases work, too. Or even a picture. Just find out something and send it to me. I'll see what I can do."

Alex hung up and went to work. She hacked into dispatch databases, called various precincts and hospitals around the city. Nothing. There was no record of any man requiring medical attention at the National Mall. No one had even called in such an event.

She looked at closed circuit monitors surrounding the area around the time Blunt alleged this incident occurred. Still nothing. Even footage of Blunt ever being there didn't exist.

After Alex exhausted all her tricks, she phoned Mallory.

"I can't find anything anywhere."

"No footage?"

"Nothing. I can't even find an image of Blunt being there."

"Maybe it didn't happen."

Alex sighed. "That's not like Blunt though. I get the feeling he trusts me implicitly."

"You're in the world of espionage, Alex. Nobody trusts anybody implicitly."

"Perhaps not, but I find it difficult to believe he made everything up."

"He could be creating a trail with you, building some alibi before he goes off the grid."

"That's not his style, either."

"Desperate times—"

"Yeah, yeah. I know. Well, thanks anyway for being willing to help. Just keep your ear to the ground for me, will ya? If Searchlight is for real, I want to know about it."

"You got it."

Alex then called Blunt to deliver the bad news. He didn't answer.

She decided to ask General Johnson if he'd ever heard of Searchlight, but he wasn't at his desk, files and documents strewn across it. Lingering longer than she should have, she glanced down at his desk and a word caught her eye on one of the papers: Searchlight.

She reached down to slide the page out of its folder when the sound of a man clearing his throat from startled her. She spun around to see the General standing there.

"Is there something I can help you with, Agent Duncan?" he asked.

"I was wondering if you've spoken with Blunt lately."

He walked past her and settled into his chair behind his desk. "Not lately. Why? Is everything all right?"

"I think so, but he asked me to look into something for him, and I haven't been able to get in touch with him."

"Well, when you do, would you let him know I'm trying to reach him?"

"I will."

She turned to leave before he spoke, halting her progress. "And Agent Duncan?"

"Yes?" she said without turning around.

"Don't ever enter my office again if I'm not in here. Understand?"

She nodded. "Yes, sir. I understand."

"Good. Now, get back to work."

Alex swallowed hard and hustled back to her desk. She wanted to see if she could find out something else, but not now. Not with General Johnson possibly knowing something about Searchlight.

The idea that such an organization existed both perplexed and excited Alex. And now she had a link, albeit a tenuous one. Even more important, the fact that perhaps General Johnson was the link complicated matters more than she'd imagined.

And she'd have to tread more carefully now.

CHAPTER 18

ON THEIR DRIVE BACK to the outfitters, Visser asked Hawk how large of an item he could sneak out of the country using his taxidermy skills. Hawk explained that it had to do with the size of the animal as well as the creativity of the client. Fully embracing his legend, Hawk shared the story of how Martin Exporter's once smuggled five hundred kilos of cocaine out of Peru and into Canada for one client.

The story almost tripped up Visser. "I thought you said you never asked what your clients ship."

"I don't. But some things are obvious." Hawk paused. "Though it could've been five hundred kilos of powdered sugar from a client who was trying to avoid paying import tax."

"If I'm going to work with you, I need to know that you will use utmost discretion in talking about us to other clients."

Thinking on his feet, Hawk looked to assuage Visser's fear. "I understand. I only tell that story because those clients are dead. They both drowned in a boating accident, if you know what I mean."

Visser knew exactly what he meant. The Diego brothers were renowned in the organized crime world for their ability to move large volumes of drugs across various borders. They'd also both drowned several years before while fishing near the Florida Keys.

Hawk never breathed their name, but he figured Visser would connect the dots.

"The Diego brothers?" Visser said. "Those are some high-end clients."

"High end, low end—it makes no difference to me. The only kind of clients I'm inclined to work with are *paying* clients."

Visser grinned. "We fit into that category."

"Good. You just let me know whenever you need help. I'll be here."

"Nothing super urgent, but I'll let you know when we're ready to move."

Hawk shook Visser's hand and patted him on the back. "It's always a pleasure meeting new business associates."

***

WHILE HE WASN'T YET CERTAIN as to Visser's reason for being in Sierra Leone, Hawk assumed it wasn't simply for the hunting. He'd been around enough lowlifes to know what they smelled like. Based on their shooting ability and other vague comments, Hawk figured Visser and his men had to be more dangerous than previously imagined. Hawk surmised that they had to be connected to Demby, if not loosely then very tightly.

Hawk texted Alex photos of Visser and his crew and asked her to look them up. In the meantime, he decided to grab something to eat at The Errant Apostrophe's again.

Ten minutes later, he was sitting at a table and looking over the menu. Hungry for some red meat, he ordered a steak.

"Our bongo steak is the best," the waitress said.

He shot her a funny glance.

"I know, I know. It's raised on a farm. I have to remember to say that first. It might cut down on all the strange looks I get."

Hawk snickered. "Someone in this part of the world is getting conscious about their food choices?"

"Never the locals. They're more concerned with survival. But you'd be surprised at who comes through these parts."

"Bongo steak it is."

She smiled. "I'll have that out for you in about twenty minutes. Ciao."

Hawk opened up the latest edition of Taxidermy Today and started thumbing through the pages. He found an article about hair-on tanning and started to learn about the "wet scrape" technique. He knew enough of the craft's basic terminology to fake it, but the more he could learn, the better. It didn't take him more than ten minutes before he was done with the article and ready to move on to something else when he noticed a American woman who'd just taken a seat at the table next to his.

With long dark hair worn up in a bun, the woman wrung her hands as she glanced around the restaurant. Hawk thought she looked down to earth and even slightly ragged, but the glimpse of her smile that he'd caught arrested him. Whatever she did, she worked hard—though Hawk suspected she would be a stunner once she cleaned off a day's worth of African dirt. He never expected to see such a beautiful woman in a location like this.

She put on a pair of spectacles, peering through them at the menu. The waitress delivered a glass of wine to her table, which went briefly ignored.

"So, Dr. Ackerman, are you going to mix it up today and order something different or are you just reminding yourself that you order the best dish on the menu every single night?"

The woman took her glasses off and smiled at the

waitress. "Carley, I think I'll take the usual."

"Excellent choice, as always," Carley said before disappearing into the kitchen.

Hawk glanced back down at his magazine, hoping to avoid eye contact.

Dr. Ackerman caught his lingering glance and leaned toward his table. "I don't believe I've seen you around here before."

Hawk looked up from his magazine and forced a smile. "Is that your best pick up line?"

The woman didn't bat an eye. "I only engage in polite conversation. Nothing good ever came of me trying to pick up a man—herniated discs, lower back pain. No. I just never pick up men."

"Quite the sharp wit, too," Hawk said with a wink. He offered his hand to her. "Oliver Martin."

She took it. "Alissa Ackerman."

"Alissa? Isn't it Dr. Ackerman?"

She nodded and leaned down, trying to peek at the title of his magazine.

He held it up. "It's just a boring taxidermy magazine."

She rolled her eyes and took a gulp of her wine.

He closed the magazine. "Sorry, it's not as noble of a profession as medicine, but it pays the bills."

"You're here hunting, aren't you?"

Hawk nodded.

"Figures. Just come and exploit the last shred of survival that's left in this country. Kill it and take it home."

"Just because I'm hunting doesn't mean I don't care."

She held up her hand. "Please. Save the self-righteous act for someone who might believe you. I'm not impressed."

Before Hawk could respond, a young boy ran into the restaurant, shouting. "Doc! Doc! We need you!" The child grabbed Dr. Ackerman by the arm and started to pull her out of her seat.

"What is it, Solomon?" she asked, almost falling out of her chair before she stood up and stopped the boy from pulling her any farther.

"The mine! The mine! It's collapsed. My father is trapped inside, and Mr. Demby is doing nothing about it."

She got up and ran.

Hawk followed her.

"Can I help?" he asked as he chased after her.

"Please. For the sake of everyone here, why don't you just get on a plane and go home?"

"I can't," Hawk said. "It sounds like there are some people who need help. Getting on a plane and escaping this place is the last thing I'd do."

"Look, Mr. Martin, you don't have to impress me.

I get it. You're altruism is unmatched."

"I'm not trying to impress anyone; I'm trying to help."

"Whatever. Get in." She pointed at the Jeep in front of them. It was covered with rust spots and plenty of caked on dirt, yet possessed four new tires.

Hawk obeyed, and Ackerman fired up the engine. Solomon hopped in the back, as did a couple of other younger boys.

"Has this happened before?" Hawk asked.

"Not since I've been here," she said, shouting over the whine of the engine and the breeze caused by her speeding along the dirt road.

Hawk played dumb. "Who runs this mine?"

"My boss," she said as she shifted gears. "I run his humanitarian organization here, SLAM."

"SLAM?"

"Sierra Leone Aid & Medical Supply Company. I know. It's a terrible acronym, but it's Africa. I'm just grateful there's someone funding my work here."

"And your boss, what's his name?"

"Musa Demby."

"Musa Demby—why wouldn't he be doing something about this?"

"He's full of contradictions, but I guess we'll find out when we get there."

"How much farther?"

She shot him a look. "The kids are in the back. With a question like that, I wonder if you'd like to join them."

Hawk chuckled and glanced at the back. They'd started with three kids, but Hawk noticed the number had now doubled.

"Six kids?" he said, pointing behind him.

She smiled. "Welcome to Africa, Mr. Martin."

A few minutes later, they arrived at the mine. Hawk had been so shocked by the multiplication of kids in the back of Ackerman's Jeep that he'd barely noticed the train of vehicles behind them. When Ackerman finally skidded to a stop at the top of the Sefadu Holdings mine, more than a dozen vehicles had fallen in line behind her. Mostly young men and boys along with a few frantic mothers and wives unloaded and joined Ackerman and Hawk as they jogged down the pit road. A few of the boys ran ahead.

Once they reached ground zero, one of the foremen held up his hands. "Whoa! Whoa! You shouldn't be here."

Ackerman pushed her way past him. "Where's Demby?"

One of the men pointed toward the western portion of the pit.

She marched in that direction, Hawk trailing behind her in an attempt to keep pace.

"What do you think you're doing?" she demanded as she interrupted Demby's conversation.

Demby looked at her. "Dr. Ackerman, it's so kind of you to join us."

"This isn't a social call. We need to get these men free."

"I'm afraid that isn't possible. It's too late for them. We're going to detonate the mine, give them a merciful ending."

"Like hell you are," she said before whistling toward the boys and pointing toward a portion of the mine. "Start working right here." She turned to Hawk. "You, come with me."

Hawk followed her closely. "You really think we can save these men by simply pulling out a few beams and pushing over some boulders?"

"I don't know, but we're sure going to try."

Hawk rolled up his sleeves and yanked a beam out of the rubble. He rushed to another pile of debris and pushed a large rock out of the way with his feet. A few moments later, an opening large enough for a man to escape through appeared. Two arms popped out of the hole.

"Help me!" the man called.

Hawk grabbed the man's arms and lifted him out.

Solomon rushed toward him before stopping short. The man wasn't his father. Instead, another young boy leapt into the arms of the man they'd just rescued.

Hawk took in the bittersweet scene. For a moment, it whisked him back in time to when he worked in the Peace Corps, giving him the satisfaction of what it felt like to help others yet the emptiness of not being able to help everyone.

A firm punch to his bicep snapped him out of his trance.

"Let's go, Mr. Martin," Ackerman said. "We've got a lot of work to do."

Hawk stooped down and noticed a small black cinch sack being pushed through a tight opening between two large support beams.

"Help me!" a man said with a gravely and raspy voice. "Take this. Just get me out."

Hawk took the bag and tossed it up and down for a moment to see how much it weighed. "What's your name?"

"Amad," the man answered. "I know it's a lot of money, but I don't care. I want to see my family again. Just get me out of here so I can be with my family again."

Hawk knew the protocol: talk about the person's family, keep them awake and alert, don't let them lose consciousness. But knowing what to do and actually achieving the desired result were two different things, ideas that didn't always materialize like people hoped.

Hawk glanced at Solomon standing near several other men who'd been rescued. He looked lost, hopeless. Hawk reached down and pulled up a stone, determined not to let Solomon live the rest of his life with that despondent look on his face.

CHAPTER 19

ONCE HE ARRIVED HOME, Blunt wasted no time in retreating to his study and pouring himself a glass of scotch. It'd been a long day, one he wished to forget quickly. But as much as he wanted to erase it from his memory, he couldn't.

He settled into his favorite chair and threw his head back, exhaling and hoping for a better tomorrow.

It can't be any worse than today, can it?

Just as he'd started to unwind, his encrypted phone rang.

What is it now?

He got up and wandered over to his desk, ripping out the charging cord from the phone.

He recognized the number. It was Thor's.

"Yeah," Blunt answered.

"I'm calling you with an update."

"What happened? Is it done? I'm watching the news and haven't seen a thing."

"No," Thor snapped. "Your intel was wrong."

"What do you mean?"

"What I mean is that I found Jepsen, identified him, posed as a hotel employee delivering room service to him, slipped him the drug—and he died of a heart attack hours later."

"So, what's the problem?"

"It wasn't Jepsen."

Blunt took another much-needed long pull on his drink. "What do you mean, *it wasn't Jepsen*?"

"Whoever had a heart attack was a body double for Jepsen." Thor took a deep breath and exhaled. "It was almost as if he was surgically altered to look like him."

"You were sure it was him?"

"Sure as I've ever been."

"So how do you know it wasn't?"

"When I returned to the kitchen, I heard one of the other employees talking about how he'd just come back from the Prime Minister's room. Someone either tipped them off or knew of our operation in advance."

"So, what's going on now?"

"Jepsen's cavalcade just left for his speech that he's scheduled to make here in Vienna in a couple of hours. They're having some kind of breakfast for diplomats before he speaks. What do you want me to do?"

Blunt finished off his glass of scotch and got up to pour himself another.

"Senator?"

"Just hang tight. I'll be in touch."

Blunt hung up and slammed his phone down on his desk. He drained the entire glass of scotch before slinging it across the room and letting out a string of expletives.

Without hesitating, he shuffled toward his window and drew the blinds.

He was wrong.

His day could—and did—get much worse.

CHAPTER 20

DEMBY BENT OVER next to Dr. Ackerman and watched as she worked frantically to pull the rubble away from one of the mine's openings. He admired her determination and grit, even if it annoyed.

"Dr. Ackerman, I think I told you it's too late. You need to back off," he said.

She stopped for a moment, wiping the sweat from her brow with her forearm. "Tell that kid right there that we're too late," she said, gesturing toward Solomon. "We just reunited him with his father. And if you had it your way, we would've just made him join the vast number of children on this continent who are fatherless for legitimate reasons."

Demby inhaled a long breath as he watched his doctor ignore his directives.

"Perhaps I wasn't clear," Demby said.

"No, you were crystal clear," Ackerman said, refusing to look up as she continued working. "But I always respond to cries for help over threats. So you can either help me free some of these men or you can get out of my way."

"I think you're forgetting who you're talking to."

Ackerman kept flinging debris away from the opening. "I haven't forgotten anything. I wish I could say the same for you. You seem to have forgotten your humanity."

"That's enough. I'm going to need you stop and instruct the rest of the people here to follow your lead."

"Good luck with that. The people who are here aren't following me; they're just being human. And I wish you'd follow their lead."

Demby grabbed her bicep and jerked her up until she was face to face with him.

"Call them off now—or I'll start detonating the charges we've set all around this mine."

She withdrew, shaking free from his grip the moment he relaxed. Briefly eyeing him, she decided to call his bluff. "Not even you could withstand the fallout from a move like that. You'd be dead before morning. Besides, you certainly wouldn't risk killing the only doctor in four hundred kilometers who could save your life if something happened to you."

Demby watched her turn her back and walk away. One of his men took a few steps in her direction before Demby called him off. "Just leave her." Then he shouted to Ackerman. "You have three hours—then," he said, lowering his voice, "*boom.*"

He watched as she frantically organized teams. One of the men with her caught Demby's eye. He'd never seen the man.

"Who is that?" Demby asked Ibrahim.

Ibrahim watched the man hoist a large beam off a pile of rubble and shove it aside.

"I think he's some taxidermist from New Zealand just here for the hunting."

"So, he just comes to my mine and starts shoving boulders aside and freeing people?"

"Maybe he met Dr. Ackerman and she asked him to come along."

"I thought she said nobody was following her."

Demby watched in silence for several more minutes as Hawk continued to move debris in machine-like fashion and efficiency.

"Does that guy ever get tired?" Demby asked. He hadn't noticed Dr. Ackerman slip up behind him.

"That's not just a guy," Ackerman snapped. "That's a *real man.*"

Demby shooed her away with the back of his hand and waited until she was working on another section of the mine thirty meters away.

"Ibrahim, I want to meet that man," Demby said. "When this is all over, bring him to me. We need to talk."

CHAPTER 21

UNSATISFIED WITH HER INABILITY to find any shred of video evidence that Senator Blunt was even at the National Mall, she tried to think outside the norms of her CIA training. With access to virtually every camera available, if Blunt had been somewhere, he would've shown up in at least one of the cameras—unless all the cameras had been hacked. And if all the cameras had been hacked, there would be a digital footprint that she could use to trace back to its origin point.

She pounded away on her computer for the better part of an hour as she tried to discover anything else about this video camera takeover. Hitting roadblock after roadblock, she realized she needed help. And she knew just who to call.

Fifteen minutes later in a small coffee shop off Massachusetts Avenue, Alex sat across a table from Kyle Kuhlman, or K-Squared as he preferred to be called. He had other aliases for his more nefarious online work, the kind that Alex's assignment required.

"Th-this is going to cost you," Kuhlman said as he looked at her handwritten note detailing the task.

"Money won't be an issue," she said.

"Who said anything about money? I just said it was going to cost you; I didn't say *what* it was going to cost you," Kuhlman said, speaking faster with each sentence. "You need to pay attention here, Agent Duncan. There are a lot of moving parts, many moving parts. And you're going to *need* me to do this. Do you understand? You're going to *need* me to do this. There's hardly a hacker alive who could execute this for you, especially since it's a special government request." He finally took a breath. "So, it's going to cost you."

"What do you mean by *that*?"

Kuhlman opened his laptop and typed furiously on the keyboard, ignoring her question.

Alex wasn't amused.

"I see you've been working on your interpersonal skills, like looking people in the eye and paying attention to what they're saying." She slammed his laptop down.

He clasped his hands together and slowly looked up at her. "I find such exercises a waste of time, especially when I can get what I want through other means."

Alex narrowed her eyes. "And what is it exactly

that you want, this thing that's going to *cost* me?"

"I want a date with you."

Alex emphatically shook her head. "Absolutely not. I couldn't imagine sitting in your apartment and playing video games all night with all your online friends. Not gonna do it."

"Hey now," Kuhlman said. "Give me a little credit here. Not *all* my dates end up like that. We can do lots of fun things that don't involve any computers or smart phones. Maybe go watch the Nationals play or catch a show downtown. Or maybe we can hang out at the National Archives, your favorite place to meet up with prospective suitors."

"Hey—what are you talking about? How do you know—?"

"K-Squared knows all, sees all. When are you going to learn that?"

Alex sighed. "Fine. I'll go on one date with you." She pointed at the instructions he'd set on the table. "Now, find out who's behind this for me. I'll give you two hours."

"Two hours? You're *loco*, girl. I can't crack this in two hours."

"What's the matter, K-Squared?" she chided. "Have you lost your magic touch?"

He glared at her. "Two hours. I'll have everything you want and more."

Alex got up and exited the coffee shop. As she was turning onto the sidewalk, she bumped into a woman.

"Sorry," Alex mumbled, but the woman didn't stop, pushing her way past Alex and scurrying down the sidewalk.

Sometimes, I just love this town.

When Alex arrived at the Metro station, she reached into her jacket pocket for her pass.

Huh? What's this?

She pulled out her pass along with an envelope addressed to her: Agent Duncan.

Alex waited to open it until she returned her office. Inside the envelope, she found a small photograph depicting Senator Blunt along with a handful of men and women, none of whom Alex recognized immediately. She flipped the picture over. Scrawled on the back was a short message, a pair of questions: "Who are these people, and what is Blunt doing with them?"

They could've been any number of groups the Texas senator met with on a regular basis: lobbyists or donors from the banking industry, oil industry, cattle industry, National Rifle Association, or a farmers' special interest group. But Alex figured whoever was asking her that question also knew she had access to facial recognition software and the most robust database in the world. So, she played along.

Alex uploaded the photo to her computer and

started the program. Of the eight figures in the photo, Blunt was identified first, almost immediately. Returning to her work, Alex decided to rely upon the software's alert system to let her know when a match was found. More than an hour later, still no more matches.

While she waited, she searched for footage of her outside the coffee shop. She needed to know whom the woman was who'd slipped this into her pocket when they collided. But that search, too, was to no avail. A large brimmed hat and oversized sunglasses ensured that the woman's identity remained hidden.

She checked the program again. Still nothing. After a couple of hours, the program's search finally ended, unable to even get a partial match.

No longer was the two-part question just written on the back of a photo.

Now, both the question and the image were seared into her brain.

CHAPTER 22

HAWK CHECKED HIS KNIFE and tightened the ankle-mounted sheath on his right leg. As a Navy Seal, he'd learned that preparation was the key to survival in any situation. Although he wasn't anticipating any conflict yet, he wasn't naive. Spreading the word around that he could handle such transactions meant that piece of information would reach the right people, the same people who were also quite dangerous.

After breakfast, he met up again outside with his guide, Ethan Jacobs. Visser leaned against Jacobs's vehicle without his previous two companions.

"Where's Soto and Perryman?" Hawk asked, rubbing his back, which was still sore from excavating all the miners the night before. Despite his initial disappointment, he'd eventually reunited Solomon with his father and satisfied his urge to help others in tangible ways.

Visser rubbed his eyes as if he were trying to wake up.

"Rough night, Visser?" Hawked asked.

A faint smile spread across Visser's lips. "You could say that. It's the same reason why Soto and Perryman aren't here."

"And it's a good thing, too," Jacobs said. "Otherwise, we wouldn't have room for another last-minute addition to our hunting party today."

"And who might that be?" Hawk inquired.

"Musa Demby, who runs the Sefadu Holdings mine, and his friend, Ibrahim," Jacobs replied.

"I think I met him last night."

Jacob's eyebrows shot up. "Really? Where at?"

"At his mine after it collapsed. We rescued over a dozen men."

"Well, I'm sure you'll have plenty to talk about then."

The roar of a Range Rover engine climbing up the hill toward them could be heard as Jacobs finished talking.

"Seems like our last two guests have arrived," Jacobs said.

Visser remained propped against Jacobs' vehicle, silent through the conversation about their two new hunting partners. "I call shotgun."

Jacobs turned toward Visser. "I'm afraid Mr. Demby will be sitting in the front seat."

Hawk winked at Visser. "It's okay. I'll let you sit in

the middle."

Demby's vehicle skidded to a stop, kicking up a cloud of dust. He and Ibrahim climbed out.

"Looks like it's my lucky day," Demby said with a wide grin as he walked toward Jacobs.

"What do you mean?" Jacobs asked as he shook Demby's hand and then gave him a hug.

"I get to go hunting with a hero," Demby said, gesturing toward Hawk. "Mr. Martin saved many lives last night at my mine. The least I can do is cover his costs for today."

Hawk shook his head. "That won't be necessary, Mr. Demby, but I appreciate the gesture. I'm just doing what any man would've done."

"I guess I'm not any man," Demby deadpanned. He then broke into a smile. "But I don't believe that for a second. *You*, on the other hand, are a very special man. What you did at my mine was amazing."

Hawk furrowed his brow. "I was just trying to help. But what are you doing here? Shouldn't you be there today? That was quite a traumatic event."

Demby laughed. "I gave the workers who'd been trapped a few days off. The rest of the employees had better double their production. A great reward will be given to them if they reach the goals I set for them."

"Such a generous man."

Demby eyed Hawk. "That's not something people

say about me very often, though I'm quite certain that your words belie the meaning behind your comment."

Hawk held out both hands and shrugged. "I'm a straight shooter, Mr. Demby. Take my comments at face value. I never meant anything underhanded by that."

"Very well then," Demby said before he turned toward Hawk. "Shall we go shoot an elephant today?"

***

DESPITE JACOBS'S DEFT SKILLS as a guide, he couldn't make Africa's most sought after trophy animals appear out of thin air. He went to all of his go-to locations and waited—but nothing. They even ventured into several areas that were ill advised due to the recent Ebola outbreak and still came up empty.

"What are we paying you for again?" Demby asked with a smirk as they traipsed through the thicket.

"For what all big game outfitter guides are paid for: entertaining stories," Jacobs replied.

"I haven't heard one all day," Hawk said.

"Well, why don't you tell us one?" Demby said as he looked at Hawk.

Hawk found a log and sat down, gesturing for his hunting companions to do likewise.

"I was in Namibia hunting leopards once when we

came upon one guarding its kill in the brush about eighty meters away," Hawk began. "The tracker motioned for me to take a shot. But just as I lined everything up, the leopard darted farther into the brush. Apparently something was more interesting to him than his kill. So, I found a tree nearby and climbed up to get a better look. But I couldn't quite determine what was happening. That's when I realized one of our trackers, Dikimbe, was missing. Dikimbe had ventured into the brush to try and draw out the leopard—and Dikimbe succeeded, but at his own demise. The leopard charged the tracker and bit him on the neck, leaving Dikimbe for dead. However, in order to get a clearer shot, I needed to climb down from the tree. The second my boots hit the ground, the cat charged me. I dodged behind a tree and just missed his leap toward me. I then emptied several shots into him and dropped him right there."

Demby chuckled. "You survived a leopard charge?"

Hawk nodded.

"Well, that's a tall tale. Perhaps you should be a guide, Mr. Martin."

Hawk held up his hand. "I swear it's the truth."

Everyone erupted into laugher, dishing out comments that suggested they didn't believe him.

"What?" Hawk said. "You think I made that up?"

"I knew Kiwis were good at lying," Demby said. "I just never knew how good."

"I swear on my mother's grave that it's true."

Demby studied Hawk. "Maybe so, but I've got a few other questions I want to ask you about. Come with me."

***

FOR THE NEXT FIFTEEN MINUTES, Demby took Hawk away from the rest of the group and grilled him about his work experience.

"I hear you are an exporter," Demby said.

"Who told you that?" Hawk asked.

"That's not important. I'm more interested in your ability to export difficult items out of certain countries."

Hawk smiled. "I haven't been stumped yet."

"How good are you?"

"Good enough to have never been caught."

Demby laughed and slapped Hawk on the back. "You sound like my kind of man. Say, would you be interested in joining us tonight for a game of cards at The Errant Apostrophe's?"

"I'd be delighted," Hawk said.

His plan was already starting to take shape.

CHAPTER 23

THE SUN HAD ALMOST DISAPPEARED on the horizon when Demby returned to his office at Sefadu Holdings. He'd endured an unproductive day of hunting, though it wasn't a complete waste of time. Despite not killing anything, he did manage to establish a rapport with Oliver Martin, the man he believed might be able to help expand his market distribution. But it was too early to tell anything.

His more immediate concern was making sure that he could get all of his illegal diamonds out of the country using SLAM as a cover. If Dr. Ackerman remained uninformed about the true contents of her latest shipment to South Sudan, everything would run smoothly. He could afford nothing less. Al Hasib took its institution of deadlines seriously—or more poignantly, they took deadlines literally.

After sorting through a few email messages from diamond consortiums in Antwerp, Demby decided to lock up for the evening and spend the rest of his night playing cards at The Errant Apostrophe's. However, his plans were delayed when he turned the key in the deadbolt and skipped down the steps—where he was met by one of his foremen and Dr. Alissa Ackerman.

"I tried to stop her, boss," the foreman said. "She wouldn't listen to me."

A wry smile spread across Demby's face as he addressed his foreman. "Don't feel bad. She doesn't listen to anybody." Then he looked at Ackerman. "So, what's this all about?"

"I think I should be the one asking you that question," she said and proceeded to hold up a small plastic bag that held about a dozen small diamonds. "I found this in the latest shipment I was preparing for South Sudan. Care to explain what's going on here?"

"It's not what it seems," Demby said. "I'm sure someone dropped it in your supplies by accident."

"People don't accidentally drop diamonds worth millions of dollars in my outbound medical supply shipment. And your workers especially don't do it."

"Believe it or not, accidents do happen here," he said as he took the bag from her. "I'll look into it."

She crossed her arms and glared at him. "Yesterday you were willing to let all those men die because it might affect your deadline. And now today you pull this stunt. This isn't a couple of anomalies; this is a trend. And it disgusts me."

Demby shooed the foreman away with the back of his hand. When Demby felt confident the man was out of earshot, he leaned in close to Ackerman.

"If you know what's good for you, you'll look the other way and go about your business of saving people's lives."

"Saving people's lives? Saving people's lives? You think that's enough to make me turn a blind eye to what you're doing? By smuggling these to God knows who, I doubt you're helping the situation. In fact, I'd be willing to bet everything that you're making it worse."

"Perhaps you're right, but without them, you couldn't do the good you do."

"Without them, I might not have to." She puffed her chest out and put her hands on her hips, doing her best to look tough. "This ends today."

Demby chuckled and looked her up and down. "Is that supposed to scare me?" Without waiting for an answer, he pulled out his pistol and pointed it at her head. "This ends when I say it does. Is that clear?"

She nodded and swallowed hard. However, she couldn't hold her tongue. "But just to be clear, just because you ask me if that's clear doesn't mean I'm going to go along with it."

He cocked the gun and jammed it into her temple. "Don't get too sassy with me. You aren't vital to my operation."

"Apparently I am, because I'm still here."

"Maybe not for long if you keep up this pace."

She cut her eyes over at the gun barrel. "I'd remove that if I were you. My lawyer has instructions to release some interesting documents to the world if I should ever die."

Demby jammed his gun into her head even harder, so much so that her entire head tilted to one side.

"You got guts, woman. I'll give you that. But it's the kind of guts that will get you killed."

He dismissed her. Fifteen minutes ago, he would've sworn that no problem he ever had would've ever been bigger than failing to deliver for Al Hasib.

He was wrong.

Dr. Ackerman was his biggest problem at the moment. But the situation could change. He'd make sure of it.

CHAPTER 24

ALEX STORMED INTO BLUNT'S OFFICE, pushing her way past his secretary. She flung an envelope at him and slumped into a chair. Propping her feet up on his desk, she nodded toward her special delivery.

"Go on," she said. "Open it. We've got a lot to talk about."

Blunt stormed around the room and closed the door behind him. "I thought I told you not to come to my office again. This is a practice that needs to end right now."

"Sorry, Senator, but this is the kind of conversation you can't have properly on the phone. I need to see your face when you open that envelope and see what's inside."

He sat down behind his desk and picked up the envelope. He shook it for a second.

"For all this drama, I would've suspect that this right here would've weighed considerably more."

"I'm not interested in your suppositions right now—only the truth about what's inside."

He glowered at her and then cut his eyes toward her feet, which were still perched on the end of his desk. "Do you mind?"

She slid her feet off his desk and let them hit the floor with a loud thud. Sitting upright, she clasped her hands together and rested them in her lap. "There. Happy now?"

Blunt pulled a letter opener out of his top right desk drawer and methodically worked the knife across the the envelope. Once he finished, he blew onto the envelope in order to flare out the sides and make it easier to pluck the contents. He pulled out the picture.

Blunt's eyes widened slightly.

"Well, this isn't what I expected?"

"What? Did you figure I unearthed some other secret?"

He forced a smile. "You don't get into the position I'm in without keeping a few secrets, both others' and your own."

She leaned forward and pointed at the picture in Blunt's hands. "So, what kind of secret is *this*?"

"There are some things it's just best you don't know about."

"Yeah, yeah. Plausible deniability. Please spare me. I want to know what's going right now."

He stood up. "Let's take a walk."

Blunt led Alex down the hall and outside. After they were a few hundred meters clear of the building, he finally spoke. "I apologize for the security measures, but you must understand that I can't be too careful."

She looked straight ahead at a woman pushing her daughter in a stroller. Once upon a time, a normal family was the life she wanted. That was before she found out how the world worked and decided she wanted to be an active participant instead of a passive bystander. She suddenly had a feeling she was about to discover again that it didn't work the way she thought it did.

"I'd rather you apologize for keeping me in the dark about what I really joined up to." She continued watching the mother toil as she pushed the carriage along.

"Firestorm still is—and always has been—the special ops program that I told you it was when I recruited you to work for it. Nothing has changed."

"Then who do you work for? Because not a single person in that photo other than you is in our facial recognition database."

"That's because I had them scrubbed."

"*You?* You had them scrubbed? Who are they, Senator? Who are you working with?"

Blunt steepled his hands, touching the tips of his

forefingers to his lips. He took a deep breath before he spoke. "What I'm about to tell you may get us both killed, but I'd rather me tell you so you'll drop it instead of ending up dead in a back alley somewhere."

"I can handle myself."

He nodded slowly. "I'm aware of that, but if these people wanted you dead, you'd be dead."

"I get it. They're powerful. What's this all about?"

"I'm part of an international alliance of powerful men and women called The Chamber. Firestorm is a legitimate black ops group, but I'm tasked with using my assets in the field to help, among other things, eliminate targets that might be less than desirable if they gain substantial power."

"So, what? Are we talking about dignitaries, terrorists, business leaders? Who are your main targets?"

He sighed. "Yes."

"What do you mean, yes?"

"I mean all of them. Anyone who might potentially gain too much power before they ascend to unreachable heights could be eliminated."

"And The Chamber acts as some type of curator for good?"

"Something like that."

Alex shook her head. "What gives you the right to determine this? Who do you think you are?"

"Alex, dear, it's no different than what you do

every day. You want to see good triumph over evil. So does The Chamber. They just have the resources to manipulate the ending."

"How old is this organization?"

"They've been around for a long time."

"And yet the world has still seen evil the likes of say, Adolf Hitler, rise to power under their watch?"

"The Chamber tried to assassinate him on more than one occasion. Unfortunately, one of its operatives didn't succeed until there had been far too much innocent blood shed."

Alex eyed him closely. "Hitler committed suicide."

"Were you there?" He chuckled. "The Chamber likes to remain invisible, which is why you've never heard of it until just now. But you'll never hear about them. When you work well in the shadows, you stay there. You understand this, don't you?"

She ignored his question. "And what happens if The Chamber gains too much power? Who's going to stop them?"

"The Chamber's mission isn't to gain power but to assure that it rests in the hands of well-meaning men and women."

"So, the prime minister of Denmark, Liam Jepsen, isn't a well-intentioned leader?"

Blunt stared at her, mouth agape. "How do you know about that?"

Alex winked at him. "I'm deeply familiar with the art of espionage, in case you've forgotten."

"Not all of our missions are affiliated with The Chamber," Blunt said, sidestepping her question. "In fact, most of them aren't. Most of what we do is about keeping this country safe and looking out for the best interests of our allies."

"So, who are all those people in that photo with you?"

"It's best that you don't know. But you're going to have to trust me on this."

Alex said nothing as she tried to grapple with what she'd just learned.

Blunt pointed at the woman who'd been pushing a stroller. She was now seated on a bench and nursing her baby. "That right there is why we do this. There are innocent people in this world who need to be protected. Without people like you and me, the world would be a far more dangerous place."

Studying the woman for a moment, Alex wondered if maybe that was the life for her and she'd been pursuing the wrong thing all this time.

He put his hands on Alex's shoulders and turned her directly in front of him. They locked eyes.

"Alex, you're damn good at what you do—and what you do matters to millions of people. They may not see it, but I promise you that you're on the right side in this war we fight in the shadows. You keep doing what you can to keep Hawk informed and safe out there, and I'll make sure that none of it is ever in vain. Deal?"

She nodded and started to turn away before he spoke again. "One more thing."

She turned toward him. "What is it, sir?"

"What did you find out about the feeds?"

"They were hacked. I had a friend look into them. Said a hacker named Bare Bones was responsible."

"And do you know where to find this Bare Bones character?"

"No, but I'll do some digging. Just know that it might be a few weeks. Hackers are only as good as their ability to remain anonymous."

"And this one must be pretty good, I imagine."

She nodded. "One of the best."

"Thanks, Alex."

They parted ways, leaving in opposite directions.

Alex glanced back at the woman who was now making funny faces at her daughter and bouncing her up and down.

She wanted to believe Blunt for both her sake and all of those nameless and faceless people that he'd mentioned. She stopped trusting people a long time ago, and she still wasn't sure what she thought about Blunt's passionate speech.

She determined right there that she was going to find out who those people were and what their true agenda was—even if it killed her.

CHAPTER 25

HAWK FINISHED HIS BEER and closely watched Visser for his poker "tell." With an average hand, Hawk would have no better than a fifty-fifty chance of winning. Almost everyone at the table would make riverboat gamblers question their own bravado in less than two hands into a game. For that reason, Hawk struggled to determine who the bluffers were and who weren't. He needed more time to decide, time which he didn't have.

"Fold," Hawk said as he pushed away from the table.

"What? You fold?" Visser said, mocking Hawk. "The man who could shoot a fly off a moving elephant's tail from eight hundred meters is going to bail?"

"Knowing when to fold is how you stay alive," Hawk said with a wink.

Visser looked down at his hand and then back up at Hawk. "In poker? Or life?"

"My advice is universal."

Hawk's exit from the table left only Visser and Soto to battle it out. Hawk wandered toward the bar where Demby was nursing a bottle of Star, Sierra Leone's most popular beer.

"Is that any good?" Hawk asked.

Demby smiled. "Better than drinking the water if you're a foreigner."

"I thought beer was always better than water, no matter what country."

"Now that is a fact, my friend."

Hawk motioned for the bartender and ordered a Star.

"Did your mine survive without you today?" Hawk asked.

"Probably did better without me."

"Yesterday was quite a challenge. I'm glad everyone survived."

"Thanks to you and Dr. Ackerman."

The bartender popped the top off a bottle of Star and then slid it to Hawk.

"She's quite *stroppy*."

Demby furrowed his brow. "*Stroppy*?"

"It's a Kiwi word. But you know—feisty, tough."

"Ah," Demby said while he nodded. "That I know. She is indeed."

Demby held up his bottle and clinked it with

Hawk's. "Cheers, mate."

Hawk smiled. "Cheers."

"So, Mr. Martin, I have a problem and was wondering if you could help me solve it."

"How can I be of assistance?"

"I understand that you are in the export business."

Hawk nodded. "Do you have need of an exporter?"

"My method for exporting some of our precious cargo out of Sierra Leone has dried up, and I need an alternative way to get some product out of the country."

"Where would I be moving this product? I'm not licensed everywhere."

"I have some clients in the Middle East. Their shipments call for extreme discretion, if you understand what I'm saying."

Hawk nodded. If he was going to portray himself as a discreet exporter, he didn't need to ask any more questions.

"I can probably help you."

Demby slapped him on the back. "You seem like a man I can trust."

"Excellent. I'm planning on being around for a few more days. Is this something we can handle while I'm still here?"

"Most certainly. Perhaps tomorrow night we can

meet to discuss how you can be of service to me."

"I'll be back from my hunting excursion then, so that will be perfect. I'll await your call. You know where I'm staying."

Demby shook Hawk's hand. "I can see we're going to get along just fine, Mr. Martin."

***

BACK IN HIS ROOM, Hawk called Alex to tell her the good news and give her a full update on what had transpired.

"So, Demby took the bait?" she asked, almost matter of factly.

"Hook, line, and sinker."

"Well, that went well."

"It's not over yet. I'm still in the dark about the weapons."

"I'm sure they'll turn up if they're there."

Hawk glanced at his watch and then outside at the star-filled sky. "Have you found out anything else about my father?"

"Nothing on him, but I've learned a few other things. When you get back, we need to talk."

"Roger that."

"Good luck, and stay in your legend."

Hawk lingered by the window for a moment, enjoying the view. With relatively few streetlights, the stars seemed to blanket the sky.

While he was caught up admiring the sparkling constellations overhead, Hawk didn't see the man crouching beneath his window slip off into the nearby forest.

CHAPTER 26

THE SUN HAD BARELY PEEKED above the horizon, but Demby had assembled every Sefadu Holdings employee for an urgent meeting just outside his office. He squinted as he glanced eastward, contemplating his next few words.

"I apologize for the inconvenience of the early start today, but I felt like I must say something before the incident two days ago begins to endanger our operation," he said as he walked around the assembled group of men. "I was under a lot of stress the other day when the mine collapsed. I wasn't acting in my right mind—and for that, I apologize. But I want to make it exceedingly clear to everyone here that I care deeply about each and every one of you. I am grateful that no one was crushed and killed in the collapse and that we can move forward. For now, we will be suspending the conversion process of our open-pit mines using block caving. There will come a day when we will venture back into those areas and mine them again. But that day is not now, nor in the immediate future."

He turned and looked down upon the rubble still sprawled out across the bottom of the open-pit mine.

"We must continue to keep safety as our priority, but also remember that production is of utmost importance. We must be safe and alive to fulfill our obligations. But if we don't fulfill our obligations, it doesn't matter how safe and alive we are; we'll all be out of a job. Is that understood?"

A few men mumbled in the affirmative.

"I can't hear you," Demby shouted.

"Yes, sir," the men responded.

"I must also remind you that if news of this collapse begins to circulate, we may all lose our jobs. Some government official may want to *inspect* what we're doing. Now, I suppose you all like being paid. Am I right?"

The men nodded.

"So, can I trust you to keep what happened here a secret between you and your families? No press, no government intrusions?"

The men all nodded again.

"Good, now let's get to work."

The men dispersed to their stations and began work for the day. Demby smiled as he watched the men scurry about in preparation for their tasks. Scanning the grounds, he caught Ibrahim's eye and gestured for him to come over.

"What is it, boss?"

"There's been a change of plans," Demby said. "Dr. Ackerman and I came to an understanding, and we're going to need to export Al Hasib's diamonds through other means."

"What did you have in mind?"

Demby stroked his chin. "Find out what you can about our new friend, Oliver Martin, the Kiwi exporter. I think he will be our best option at this point. He seems capable and willing—two traits I find highly desirable."

"Do you think he'll be a new permanent answer to our problem?"

Demby shrugged. "I see him more as a temporary solution at best, if you know what I mean."

He trudged up the stairs to his office and placed a call to a Mr. Martin.

CHAPTER 27

IF THERE WAS A HEAVEN ON EARTH, Senator Blunt suspected it would be located somewhere near Carrizo Springs, Texas. Blunt adored Hog Heaven, his sprawling ranch nestled deep in the southwest Texas woods less than an hour away from the Mexican border. His hunting lodge was modest by Texas standards, but at five thousand square feet with fifteen bedrooms, it could host a substantial party.

However, for his impromptu trip back, Blunt wasn't interested in seeing every bed filled for a roaring weekend of fun. And hunting was the last thing on his mind. This time, he went to Hog Heaven for privacy, the kind of extreme privacy that wasn't available anywhere in D.C.

An elderly gentleman meandered through the hallway and stared at the pictures on the wall of statesmen, athletes, and various other celebrities.

"Who's this guy?" the man asked Blunt.

Blunt took a sip of his coffee and shuffled out of

the kitchen toward his guest. A wide smile broke across his face. "That's Nolan Ryan, the greatest pitcher to ever come out of Texas."

"What sport is that? Baseball?" the man asked. His question betrayed his nationality almost as much as his English accent.

"That's right. America's pastime."

"I thought that was football," the man said with a chuckle. "Baseball is such a boring sport."

"You better be glad that Nolan Ryan isn't here to hear you say that. He might just pummel you like he did Robin Ventura when that fool charged the mound. Ryan beat the ever-lovin' daylights out of him as a forty-something year old."

The man scoffed. "You Americans and your violence. Such a needless spectacle."

Blunt held up his index finger. "Not always. You know that better than anyone."

Lord Williams was a British businessman who held unprecedented sway with the prime minister even though he remained relatively unknown to the public. While persnickety at times, Blunt tolerated it from his closest confidante in The Chamber.

"So, why are we here, Lord Williams? Why did you think we needed to come all the way out into the Texas hills to talk?"

Williams took a deep breath before speaking. "I'm

concerned, Senator."

"About what? My list of things I'm concerned about stretches across the Atlantic and back several times."

"I didn't drag you out here to talk about my prostate, that's for certain."

"What is it then?"

"I'm afraid there's a mole within The Chamber."

"A mole?" Blunt paused. "I can't say I'd be completely surprised by this."

Williams cocked his head. "No? You have your suspicions as well?"

"If what happened in Vienna isn't proof, I don't know what is."

"I agree. However, that was your assignment. You're aware of The Chamber's policy for failed missions, aren't you?"

Blunt nodded and looked out the window at the security guard patrolling the grounds. "Which is why I'd never sabotage my own mission in any way." He paused and narrowed his eyes. "Are you insinuating what I think you're—?"

"Yes, I am."

Blunt slammed his fist on the counter. "How dare you drag me out here to accuse me of such a thing, especially when you know how much I've sacrificed for this organization."

Williams gazed out the window. "Your son was

hardly a sacrifice. He was a ticking time bomb."

Blunt fiddled with the watch on his wrist. He remained silent, seething as he glared at Williams.

"Senator, I know you're aware of The Chamber's Monitors. Nothing gets past them. They are trained to ensure that integrity remains within our organization. And you've sent up red flags with some of your behavior lately, especially the Vienna mission."

"What do you want me to do? Resign?"

Williams shrugged. "It'd be a first for The Chamber, but I suppose it's an option the board would be willing to consider."

"Well, you can forget it. I'm as loyal as the day is long. And as we like to say in the South, you're barkin' up the wrong tree."

"The truth is you haven't been the most helpful to the organization. Besides, you're only one election away from selling used cars in Dallas again or, if you're lucky, playing golf for the rest of your days at that country club you're always blathering about."

"I've got four more years until I'm up for re-election, and my approval ratings have never been higher."

Williams looked out the window again. "Until the next scandal comes to light. If you lose your standing with the defense committee and—along with it—your funding, you've outgrown your usefulness."

"We're all prone to losing our influence should the

perfect storm occur."

"But not everyone is so reckless in how they handle their affairs."

"Perhaps, but I'm also the only one who could handle that situation in Botswana two years ago. Without me, who knows where The Chamber would be today."

Williams glanced outside again and then back to Blunt. "I suspect that was only to win our trust."

"I don't think this conversation is productive any more. If you think that I'm a mole, then you need to bring me before the council and let them decide."

"They already have."

Blunt furrowed his brow and stared at Williams. Before Blunt could say another word, out of the corner of his eyes he saw one of his guards stagger to the ground. A faint smile broke across Williams's face.

Without hesitating, Blunt dove to the ground and hid behind his counter in the kitchen as bullets tore through his lodge. Once the bullets stopped, the sound of a stool scraping across the floor followed by purposeful footsteps terrified Blunt even more.

Shaking his head, Williams looked down at Blunt. "Look at you, cowering like a gutless coward. We gave you one task, J.D.—one task. And you couldn't even complete it." Williams pulled out a gun and pointed it at Blunt while pacing around in a small circle. "So, here we are."

Blunt held up his hands to shield his face. "Please, Lord Williams. You have to believe me. Someone is setting me up."

Williams laughed. "I expected you to try and persuade me otherwise, but I certainly didn't expect you to beg."

Desperate, Blunt grabbed Williams's free arm, tugging on his wrist. "Please, you've got to believe me."

Williams felt a prick on his arm and shook free, jamming his gun into the back of Blunt's head. "Time for you to—"

Williams collapsed before he started convulsing on the kitchen floor. Within seconds, he was dead.

Blunt collected the English statesman's gun and shoved it into his belt. He then grabbed the body and dragged it to the front door. Propping the body up, Blunt swung the door open. He made Williams appear to wave outside at the shooter.

The shooter let his guard down and stepped out from behind a row of bushes.

Blunt dropped Williams and opened fire on the man who'd strafed his cabin. The man tumbled to the ground.

Blunt looked down at Williams's body. For sure, Blunt would have some explaining to do, but he was confident he'd emerge the media's inquiries unscathed.

After all, it wouldn't be the first time he'd have to ask the local medical examiner for a favor.

CHAPTER 28

DESPITE THE CIRCUMSTANCES, Hawk tried to enjoy the beauty of Africa. It wasn't every day that he had the opportunity to venture into such majestic country and soak in one of the perks of his job. He'd begun to settle into his legend as Oliver Martin, Kiwi taxidermist and exporter of unique items, so much so that he started to wonder if it might be a job he'd prefer over covert operative.

During their hunt, they encountered three of Africa's big five—a black rhinoceros, a cap buffalo, and a leopard—but never got off a shot. Jacobs told them that seeing a leopard in Sierra Leone was increasingly rare and they ought to be grateful for the opportunity to see it, even if they didn't have the chance to take a shot at the animal. Hawk knew he could've at the very least felled the Cape buffalo but was content to just see the animal in its natural habitat.

After they returned to the outfitter's facility, Hawk showered and changed. He wanted to get to The Errant Apostrophe's well in advance of Demby in order to properly scout out the location in case things went awry.

Hawk took a seat at the bar and ordered a Star beer before a man sat down next to him.

The man glanced at Hawk's beer before chuckling. "It tastes like piss, but what can you do? We're in Africa."

"Oliver Martin," Hawk said, offering his hand.

The man shook it. "Jay Collier."

Hawk's eyes shot up. "*The* Jay Collier? The former quarterback for the Florida Gators?"

Collier grinned and held his hands out. "The one and only, in the flesh."

"I'm from New Zealand, but I'm a closet fan of American college football. I seem to remember a game where you almost single-handedly beat Auburn."

"That was a long time ago—but it doesn't take much to beat Auburn . . . as long as they aren't cheating."

Both men laughed heartily at Collier's comment.

"So, what brings you here to Sierra Leone?" Collier asked, gesturing toward Hawk's drink. "I know it's not the beer."

Hawk chuckled. "Definitely not the beer. I'm just a Kiwi taxidermist who came here for the hunting. What about you?"

"I've got a similar story, but I never left."

"How long have you been here?"

"Going on five years next month."

Hawk sipped his beer. "And you're still alive."

"I know. Hard to believe, isn't it?"

"So, what do you do here now?"

"I work with a hunting outfitter and serve as a guide. Beats real work."

Hawk laughed. "So true."

"So, how has your hunting been?"

"I killed a duiker earlier this week."

"Bravo. Those little buggers aren't easy to find these days, not to mention the government frowning on eating them due to the Ebola outbreak."

Hawk nodded. "I swear, if I hear the word *Ebola* one more time—"

Collier stood up. "Come with me. I want to show you something."

Unconcerned, Hawk stood up and followed his new acquaintance.

"I know who you are and why you're here," Collier said in a low growl.

"What?" Hawk said, playing coy. "What are you talking about?"

Collier chided him about his hunting exploits before he explained to Hawk that he'd heard everything outside his bedroom window the night before and that he knew he was CIA.

"You sure as hell ain't a taxidermist—and I'm going to need some cold hard cash to not run to Demby with this. I know I'll be rewarded handsomely by him."

Hawk continued his act as they trudged away from the bar, frustrating his captor. Tired of Hawk's charade, Collier put a knife to Hawk's throat.

When they walked past an outhouse, Hawk seized his opportunity to put an end to Collier's shenanigans. Needing only a few moves, Hawk immobilized Collier, knocking him out cold. Hawk glanced around to see if anybody had noticed them. He appeared to have escaped without being seen. Due to Collier's aggressive and threatening nature, Hawk had only one option: eliminate the man who could blow his cover.

Hawk positioned Collier on the toilet in the outhouse and slit his wrist. It'd look like a suicide. Hawk grabbed Collier's wallet.

Or a robbery.

Either way, he wouldn't be a suspect and his legend would remain intact.

Hawk knew he'd have to be more vigilant as the bloodletting was about to begin.

Slipping back into the bar, Hawk sat down on a stool before his phone rang. It was Demby, and he wanted to meet.

CHAPTER 29

ALEX CALLED HAWK to let him know she was working all her back channels to set up a way to smuggle Demby's diamonds to the U.S. She'd reached out to several of her West African operatives from her CIA days to find out who would be reliable contacts to help him escape the country. She needed a fast and safe route out of Sierra Leone, one that wasn't fraught with palms that required exorbitant greasing. With no possibility of a military extraction, Alex had to make sure Hawk could exit the country swiftly and safely. And on a continent where those two words described hardly anything but gazelles and armored Range Rovers, it was a daunting task.

"How did things go today?" she asked.

"I'm on my way to meet Demby—but it hasn't been easy."

"Trouble in paradise?"

"I wish it was only trouble. Some guy accosted me in the bar and said he knew who I was. He tried to drag me out into the woods and threaten me before I had to kill him."

"Better him than you."

"That's how I see it."

"Well, I wanted to let you know I've got your escape route set up. You can't get out through Freetown. You're going to have to drive to Kankan, Guinea. I'll forward you all the details, but I've got a missionary pilot there who'll fly you to Accra, where you can catch a commercial flight back to the states."

"And what about the diamonds?"

"I've got an exporter in Accra who works with the CIA who's willing to take on the diamonds for you."

"Sounds like you've been busy, Alex."

"You could say that."

"How's Blunt been?"

"I haven't heard from him in a few days."

"Is that unusual?"

"When we're in the middle of an operation, it is. I know he went to his ranch in Texas, but I haven't heard from him since he left."

"See if you can reach him. He needs to know what's going on here. If I pull this off, this will seriously cripple Al Hasib's operation for a while."

"Let me try again. Hang on."

Alex put Hawk on hold while she dialed Blunt's number. Still nothing. She then called his chief of security. Straight to voicemail.

"Hawk?" she said.

"I'm here."

"Still not gettin' anything from him. I'm starting to get a little bit worried, since he's usually checked in or called me back by now after I left him a couple of messages. I even asked General Johnson, and he hasn't heard from him either."

Hawk sighed. "Well, relay to him what's going on for me, will you? I know this will be a big feather in his cap."

"Especially if you can find those weapons."

"Just give me some time. I'm working on it."

CHAPTER 30

HAWK PULLED INTO THE gravel parking lot in front of Sefadu Holdings, kicking up a cloud of dust that hung thick in the evening air. He climbed out of his vehicle and strode toward the small office building. The window air conditioning unit hummed, forming a strange melody with the nocturnal animals calling out into the night.

Hawk tapped on the window and waited. In a matter of seconds, Ibrahim greeted him and ushered him inside.

Demby stood in the center of the room with a grin on his face. "Mr. Martin, it's so good to see you. We have much to talk about."

Hawk smiled back. "So I understand."

"Please," Demby said as he gestured to a chair in the corner of the room across from a desk, "have a seat."

Hawk sat down and took a deep breath. While he enjoyed engaging with the enemy in close quarters, this environment felt claustrophobic. More coffin than level playing field. If anything went wrong, he couldn't see himself escaping alive.

"So, do you think we can do some business?" Hawk asked.

Demby nodded. "If I didn't, you wouldn't be here right now."

"Well, how can I help you?"

Demby leaned back in his chair. "Sefadu Holdings has some sensitive product that requires export. With some of the recent uprisings, it's become very difficult to move our product out of the country to some of the unique locations we do business with."

"And that's where I come in?"

"We were hoping you could provide a solution for us—at least you intimated as much."

Hawk nodded. "Let's dispense with the vague talk, Mr. Demby. Are we talking diamonds?"

Demby nodded.

"In that case, I can assure you that I'll have no problem moving your product for you. I've moved hundreds of similar products between countries using my taxidermy business and have never even had a client searched twice in customs."

A faint smile spread across Demby's face. "Tell me more."

"It's a very simple process. I create an animal that

has space inside. I work some of my magic—and even the best customs agent with his high-powered scanner will never be the wiser. And that's a promise."

"Who transports the product?"

"It's your product, so naturally you do. That way you don't have to worry about taking your eyes off your prized possession. You can check the stuffed animal that's serving as a mule for your product. Then you pick up the animal at baggage claim—and no one has a clue what you're really doing." Hawk eyed Demby closely. "Do you have someone who can fly with your product?"

Demby nodded. "I do. And this sounds easy enough. What's your fee?"

"Two-hundred-fifty-thousand U.S. dollars per transaction. I trust that won't be a problem."

"Not at all. But we're kind of in a hurry. How quickly can you make this happen?"

"If you buy the ticket, I can have you heading out of the country tomorrow on a plane? Fast enough for you?"

Demby smiled again. "Most definitely."

Hawk offered his hand, which Demby shook. "So, where do I sign?"

Before Demby could answer, he was approached by one of his lieutenants who proceeded to whisper in Demby's ear before walking away and standing against the wall.

Demby glared at Hawk.

"Do we have a problem?" Hawk asked.

"I think we do, Mr. Martin," Demby said, drawing his gun. "Now, who are you?"

Hawk put his hands up. "We must have a misunderstanding of sorts. I-I don't know what this is all about."

"I'm quite certain you do."

Hawk cocked his head to one side.

"I wish I could help you, but if this is how it's going to be, I'll be leaving now." Hawk made a move toward the door.

"You aren't going anywhere."

Hawk fumbled for the right words. "Like I said, I'm afraid this has been a—a big misunderstanding."

"I'm afraid it hasn't. I've been cynical about you for several days now, while everyone around me convinced me that you were legitimate. Well, apparently you aren't."

Hawk put his hands in the air. "Regardless of what you might *think* you know about me, I'm still your best bet to move your product. Now, if you have specific questions, just give me a chance to explain."

"I have little tolerance for people like yourself."

"I swear, whatever information you're getting about me that's making you pull a gun is bad information. My name is Oliver Martin, and I'm a taxidermist from New Zealand."

Demby walked over to Hawk and pistol-whipped him in the back of the head, sending Hawk to the floor.

"Tie him up. We'll deal with him later."

CHAPTER 31

BLUNT SHIFTED IN HIS SEAT once his private jet reached cruising altitude. Ever since the attack at his ranch, he hadn't had a moment to relax as he remained on edge the entire time. Convincing Dimmit County's Justice of the Peace, Ernest Fowler, to avoid an investigation into the deaths was no small task. Fowler happened to have a weakness for hunting, and Blunt leveraged that to avoid not only an investigation into the deaths of the two men outside his cabin along with Lord Williams but also any future potential investigations. The cover story would be a poker game gone awry. The men were drunk and armed—and it didn't end well for any of them. The media would lap it up, using the story to push its agenda for stricter gun control and neglecting to investigate the claims. Fowler assured Blunt that all three bodies would be cremated and that he'd be cleared of any wrongdoing by setting the time of death well after he'd taken flight back to D.C.

But those were immediate concerns that he'd dealt with already. The more troubling concerns were the ones surrounding The Chamber and figuring out who he could trust. He might be able to trust his ex-wife, but he doubted she would even speak to him. He wasn't even sure if he could trust his own team at Firestorm or any of the aides in his office.

For the first hour of the flight, he didn't want to call anyone. But he had to. Knowledge was power, and he needed to know what was happening with Thor.

Blunt's most recent conversation with his No. 2 operative revolved around a blown assignment. Obviously, the Danish prime minister, Liam Jepsen, had been tipped off that an attempt would be made on his life, and The Chamber believed Blunt was the mole. For The Chamber to reach such a conclusion, Blunt realized that there was only one person who could've convincingly scapegoated him to everyone else.

Blunt called General Johnson to see if he could get an update on Thor. The only way Blunt would be able to salvage his reputation with The Chamber was if Thor succeeded. And with someone pulling strings within the organization and tipping off Jepsen, Blunt saw his assignment as one that consisted of insurmountable odds.

"Have you heard from Thor yet?" Blunt asked.

"Not yet, but just give it some time," Johnson answered. "When he's on these missions, I sometimes don't hear from him for days. I wouldn't be too worried if I were you."

"Well, I am. I'm beginning to be concerned that he's been set up."

"What makes you think that, Senator?"

"For starters, there are too many strange coincidences happening. If Liam Jepsen didn't know about a pending assassination attempt on his life, why would he have a body double? He's the prime minister of Denmark, for God's sake. It's not like they'd be out to get him."

"Have you watched the news lately? He's not the most popular leader there."

Blunt scoffed at Johnson's suggestion. "He's a political leader in Europe. The last leader beloved by any constituency with any overwhelming consensus on that continent was Hitler."

"Churchill was popular."

"Not before he was wildly unpopular, and he always had stout detractors."

"Well, no matter what the case, it's clear to me that he wasn't universally beloved by the Danes."

Blunt sighed. "But that doesn't mean he'd be worried about an attempt on his life. To have a body double? That's a whole other level of paranoia. Something's just not right about that situation."

"Perhaps, Senator, but like I said, Thor is diligent and will get the job done. Don't you worry. He'll get his man."

"I hope you're right," Blunt said before he hung up.

My life depends on it.

CHAPTER 32

WHEN HAWK REGAINED CONSCIOUSNESS, he didn't know where he was. Demby's goons had bound Hawk's hands and feet with rope, tethering him to a pole in the middle of a small room that appeared to be a pantry of sorts. Hawk could barely make out his surroundings, but the light seeping beneath the door was sufficient enough to see a general outline of the environs.

He shook off his grogginess and sat upright when he heard muffled voices approaching. The voices grew louder before one voice rose to a discernible level.

"I said *enough*," a man roared. "You stay right there, and I'll get it for you."

The sound of keys rattling in the doorknob gave Hawk hope that he might be able to find a sympathetic ear. The door swung open, and light from outside flooded the room. Hawk took a deep breath to yell for help when he stopped short upon seeing the guard holding a gun in one hand along with his index finger on the other hand tightly pressed to his lips.

"If you want to stay alive, you'll save your breath," the man said.

Hawk slowly exhaled.

"I'll be back to deal with you soon enough," the guard said in a low voice as he slammed the door behind him.

Hawk knew the protocol. Stick to the script; stay alive. But he couldn't be blamed if he wanted to leave it behind for a few minutes and freelance. It wasn't his best plan, but it might work—just as soon as he was unshackled. In the meantime, he had few options.

The voices outside became muted tones again, even as Hawk strained in the direction of the door to hear what was being discussed on the other side.

The footfalls on the concrete floor grew faint until Hawk heard another door slam shut.

With no one around to hear him, Hawk seized the opportunity to try and free himself, but the knots were too tight. He wasn't going anywhere.

After his wrists started to bleed from attempting to wriggle free, he stopped trying and slumped on the floor. That's when he heard another set of footsteps, though not nearly as heavy as the last ones.

When the door flew open and the lights flickered on, Hawk stared up at the person above him as a smile broke across his face.

"Dr. Ackerman," he said in a whisper, "do you think you can help me out?"

She shut the door and knelt down next to him. "What are you doing in here?"

"I was about to ask you the same thing."

"This isn't the time for joking around."

Hawk furrowed his brow. "Do I look like I'm joking?"

"I'm not sure what you're doing, but helping you is likely going to get me in trouble."

"I think you're the one in trouble. Demby isn't who you think he is."

"He's a compassionate man who's funded my work out of the goodness of his heart."

"That's bullshit, and you know it."

She sighed. "Fine. Whatever. You got me. I know who he is."

"And you're not going to help me?"

"Look, I want to help you, but Demby will kill me if he finds out I assisted you—and I don't mean that in some metaphorical sense either. He'll shoot me in the head or kill me some other way. No matter what he decides, it won't be pleasant."

Hawk raised his hands as much as he could. "So you're just going to leave me in here like this?"

"I'm sorry. I don't have a choice."

"You always have a choice. You're just afraid to

make the right one."

"If I help you, I understand that there will be thousands upon thousands of people who won't get helped around here as a result of Demby's generosity. Who am I to let all those people perish just because you're tied up in a closet? If you thought about it for a moment, you'd realize that it's the right decision, the only decision."

Hawk shook his head. "There you go with a classic either-or decision. What if you could have it both ways?"

"I'm listening."

"I don't want to get into all the details now, but this isn't about deciding between me and all those people here you serve. It's about choosing to do the right thing no matter what."

"Can you guarantee me you'll make sure SLAM remains funded?"

"I'll do you one better: I'll make sure it gets endowed."

"Endowed? How can you—?"

"Never mind the details. I'll tell you all about it later. In the meantime, can you just cut me free? We're losing valuable time here."

Dr. Ackerman slid a knife out of her back pocket and began slicing through the ropes binding Hawk. She was so busy hacking her way through the ropes that she didn't hear the footsteps that snuck up on both of them.

The door swung open and Ackerman turned around in horror, looking up at Demby, whose looming body nearly blocked all the light from outside.

"What have we here?" he said as he circled Ackerman and Hawk. "Your own little version of The Great Escape, I see. Too bad it's not going to work."

"It's not what it looks like," Ackerman stammered.

Demby backhanded Ackerman. "Do you think I am that stupid? Do you think I'm going to believe any lie that you've concocted to save yourself? I know exactly what this looks like—and I know exactly what's going on here."

"Please, sir," Ackerman pleaded.

Demby ignored her and turned toward Hawk. "And you," Demby said as he held up a small comlink in his hand, "look what I found in your ear." He paused for a moment before he crushed it between his thumb and forefinger. "You won't be talking to anyone else tonight."

"I swear, you're getting the wrong idea," Ackerman said, taking another tact.

"Silence, Doctor. I know what you're up to—and you're not going to like what I'm about to do next."

CHAPTER 33

ALEX JUMPED WHEN HER PHONE buzzed on her desk. She leaned over the screen to see who was calling. It was Senator Blunt.

"Good to hear from you, Senator," she said. "I was beginning to get concerned."

"I can handle myself."

"I never doubted you could."

"Have you heard from Hawk? Does he have a location for the missiles yet?"

"Not since I last spoke with him. Right now, I'm trying to track him. He's gone off the grid for the moment."

"Update me the minute you hear from him. I need to know what's going on with those missiles."

"Will do."

She hung up and started typing furiously on her keyboard. Someone had repositioned her satellites, and she wasn't excited about the prospect of re-tasking satellites, a chore that wasn't as simple as it looked in the movies. The hulking chunks of metal orbiting the earth didn't just magically move around at the whims of some programmer sitting at a computer. It took time to move a satellite into position to see a certain segment of the grid.

She picked up her phone and dialed General Johnson.

"Do you know why my satellites are out of whack this morning?" she asked.

"Beats me. I know there were navigational issues with a few of them this morning, but I've got no idea if any you were handling were in that batch."

"I wish people around here would let me know that kind of pertinent information. I'm not here for my health."

"I'll try to make sure you're better informed next time."

"One more thing, General Johnson," Alex said and then paused. She wanted to ask him about Searchlight, but she doubted it'd do much good over the phone. She needed to ask him in person.

"What is it, Agent Duncan?"

She decided to ambush him later instead. "You have a good day, sir."

Alex drummed her fingers on the desk while she waited for the satellite to get into position. After a few minutes, she decided to go get a cup of coffee around the corner. Her former supervisor at the CIA used to chide Alex for her determination to sit and stare at the screen when a satellite was in the process of being repositioned.

"A watched pot never boils," one of her supervisors at the CIA once told her, "and a re-tasked satellite never moves."

Alex snickered. "I saw them move three times last week."

"Never spoil a good idiom."

She decided to take a break and go see Cookie. It'd been a few days since she visited The Golden Egg, and she needed to vent to someone.

"The usual, doll?" Cookie asked the second Alex's fanny hit the seat at the bar.

"You know me, Cookie. Once I get in my routine . . ."

He winked at her. "Coming right up."

Alex glanced at her watch. She estimated she had about twenty minutes before the satellites were in position to monitor Hawk. Satisfied that she had enough time, she turned her attention to Cookie, who had just cracked the last egg and tossed it onto the grill.

Wiping his hands on his apron, Cookie turned around and eyed Alex closely.

"So, what is it now? Men problems?"

Alex chuckled. "*Men* problems? I'd be ecstatic if there was just *one man*—and I was having problems with him."

He put his hands on the counter and leaned forward,

shrugging before he spoke. "Well, you had that look."

"A look?"

"Yeah, that one you get when there's something deeply troubling you. And usually, it's only about men."

A faint smile spread across her lips. "Cookie, you know me about as well as any man does."

"Well ain't that a shame." He spun around and jostled the eggs before he turned back to face Alex. "You're gonna make a lucky man very happy one day. You mark my words."

"Thanks, Cookie. You're always so encouraging."

"That's what I do."

She watched him transfer the food from the grill to her plate, which he slid in front of her.

"That and make a mean plate of eggs."

She took a few bites before she got Cookie's attention. "Let me ask you a question."

"Shoot."

"If you suspected someone was lying to you, how would you trap them into telling you the truth?"

He furrowed his brow. "Are you sure you don't have men problems?"

"Positive."

"Well, all right then." He took a deep breath. "If it were me, I'd probably say something like, 'Alice, I know you've been cheating on me with Frank.' And then sit back and watch the person try to wriggle out of it. At least, that's what my third ex-wife did to me when she caught me gambling."

"Three ex-wives, Cookie? And you are just itching to give me relationship advice?"

He held up his left hand, showing all his fingers. "Five actually, but who's counting. Now trust me when I say this, but the majority of the advice I give is what *not* to do—and it's all based off personal experience."

"So, what should I *not* do if I want this person to admit the truth?"

"You should confront them."

"Even if it costs me my job?"

"There's little value in working with people you can't trust, especially someone like you who's in the finance industry."

Alex forced a smile. She hated lying to Cookie, but she realized it came with the territory. He was a friendly—and lonely—chef at a diner, completely harmless. Yet she lied to everyone she knew about what she did and who she really was. She'd developed such a knack for it that sometimes she started to believe her own cover story was true.

She gobbled down the breakfast food that served as her lunch before returning to the office.

Her watch buzzed the second she sat down, and she realized the satellite re-tasking process had been completed.

"All right. Let's see what we got here."

She put her comlink in her ear and tried to connect with her asset.

"Hawk, come in," she said. "This is Duncan. Do you read me?"

Nothing.

She tried again. Still nothing.

In a matter of seconds, she had the comlink's most recent location, though diagnostics showed that it was no longer functioning. She cross-referenced the location with intel she had on Demby and realized that Hawk had been—or still was—at a facility owned by Sefadu Holdings.

"Hawk, come in," she yelled.

Silence over the airwaves.

After five minutes of trying to raise Hawk to no avail, she decided to track his cell phone, which had also been located in the same facility. But, like the comlink, it had ceased responding about an hour ago.

She zoomed in on the location and identified several armed guards heading into the building.

"Hawk, Hawk! Come in. Please."

She had eyes on the facility, but as far as Hawk was concerned, she was dark—and so was he. This time, all she could do was hope that he could get out of this predicament by himself.

CHAPTER 34

HAWK HEARD DEMBY WHISTLE for his guards
to administer some punishment. Dragging Hawk and
Ackerman out of the small closet and into an open
warehouse space, the guards followed Demby's instructions. They tied Hawk face-first to a large support
beam before one of the guards pulled out a whip and
started lashing Hawk, sending Ackerman into hyster-
ics.

"Stop it, Demby. Just stop it," she screamed.

He turned to her and smiled, flashing his pearly
whites interspersed with several gold teeth. "This is
the price of your betrayal, Doctor. But don't worry—
you're next."

Hawk tried to ignore the searing pain emanating
from his back and spreading across the rest of his
body. Concocting an escape plan was the only mental
diversion he had. He noticed the sharp edges on the
support beam and started to work his plan.

Following the next blow to his back, Hawk wailed

and dropped to the floor.

"Get up," one of the guards said as he grabbed Hawk around his shirt collar and yanked him back to his feet.

Another lash, another collapse to the floor, another jerk to his feet. The cycle continued for about a minute until Hawk was satisfied the rope was sufficiently frayed. One strong tug and he'd be free. All he had to do now was endure the pain and wait for the right moment.

Demby laughed smugly at the scene. "Mr. Martin, I admire your tenacity and your commendable attempt to infiltrate my organization, but I'm afraid in the end it's going to be nothing more than a footnote on your way to an untimely death on our dangerous continent. Perhaps you'll slip into crocodile-infested waters and be eaten alive or trampled by an elephant during a stampede while hunting or killed by a band of marauders looking to strip the wealth from an unsuspecting foreigner. The possibilities are almost endless."

Demby held his hand up to halt the beating. He walked slowly toward Hawk before stopping just inches from his face.

"Do you think I'd be so unprepared as to not have alternative ways to transport my diamonds to their desired locations? Your scheme might be quicker, but there are other ways out of Sierra Leone. The threat of death can be a powerful persuader."

"Speaking of death, if you're going to kill me, I advise you to do it now and make it quick."

Demby threw his head back and guffawed. "You're not in any position to be telling me what to do."

Hawk glanced over at Ackerman and winked. With one ferocious pull, Hawk severed his bindings and hit Demby in the throat. Demby staggered backward before Hawk followed up with a flying kick to Demby's chest.

Surprised by Hawk's sudden freedom, the guards scrambled to get into a position to shoot him. With Demby nearby, they appeared reluctant to shoot out of fear of hitting their leader.

Hawk scurried behind another beam, utilizing it as a shield. He lunged for Demby's body and dragged it back as the guards remained hesitant to take a shot. Hawk delivered a knockout blow to Demby's face before scavenging his belt holster for a knife and hand-gun.

With his back against the beam, Hawk craned his neck around the corner to assess the situation. Nothing had changed. One guard held Ackerman, another held a whip. Ibrahim and another guard stood about ten feet away from the other two—all four of them out in the open.

Hawk eased to his feet by bracing his back against

the beam and stayed out of sight from the guards. With one swift throw to his left, he took aim with the knife at one of the guards next to Ackerman. Before the knife found its target, Hawk spun to his right and shot both Ibrahim and the other guard in the head. By the time he turned back left, the guard holding Ackerman tightened his grip around her neck and fought with her to move backward. He dragged her behind a stack of wooden boxes.

Seizing the opportunity to regain a tactical advantage, Hawk snuck behind a pile of cargo. He worked his way across the room and used the cargo lying around as a shield as he dashed from one hiding place to another. After about a minute, he'd climbed on a heavy-duty shelving unit, positioning himself above the guard and Ackerman.

While Hawk would've preferred to shoot the guard, grab Ackerman, and escape, he refused to abandon the mission. He needed to know Demby's plan for exporting the diamonds, information Hawk figured would be easier and quicker to extract from a guard than from Demby.

Hawk took a deep breath and leapt onto the guard. Under the weight of Hawk, the man crumpled to the ground. Panicked, he started firing his gun, hitting Ackerman in the arm.

She wailed in pain, writhing on the floor.

"It's okay, Doc. I'm gonna get you out of here," Hawk said, breaking from his legend.

Hawk turned his full attention to the man pinned beneath him. "Where are the diamonds?"

"I-I don't know. They never tell me anything."

Hawk's eyes narrowed. "The way I see it, you've got three options. You can walk out of here, crawl out of here, or end your miserable existence on this very spot. It all depends on how you answer my next question. So, I'll ask it again: Where are the diamonds?"

"They're headed for a train depot along that border that connects with Monrovia," the guard answered.

"Where can I find this train?" Hawk said.

The man didn't answer.

Hawk jammed his gun into the man's kneecap. "Remember when I said one of your options might be to crawl out of here?"

The man nodded.

"Where is this train?"

"It's a three-hour drive south of here on the Manu River. You'll never make it in time."

Hawk punched the man in the face, knocking him out.

Grabbing the guard's gun and knife, Hawk rearmed himself and rushed over to Ackerman, who was reclining against a box several feet away.

"You're coming with me. You need help," Hawk said.

She waved him off. "I'm fine. Just give me a minute. I'll get out of here on my own."

"You know more guards will be coming, don't you?"

Hawk didn't wait for her answer, instead scooping her up and tossing her over his shoulder.

"What are you doing?" she said.

"Making sure you get out of here alive. Ethan Jacobs will take care of you," Hawk said as he ran for the door.

"The outfitter? He's in Demby's pocket. You might as well be carrying me to my death."

"If I leave you here, you're as good as dead anyway. Besides, I pegged Jacobs as a man who will do anything if the price is right."

"And you're betting my life on the fact that the price you're going to pay him is high enough?"

"Would you rather bet it on the goodwill of these goons?"

"I guess I'm gambling either way."

Hawk froze as he scanned the room near the door.

"What is it?" she asked.

"Demby. I was going to finish him, but he's gone."

"He's like a cockroach, I swear. You're not the first person to come in here and try to kill him."

"If I'd tried to kill him, he'd already be dead."

***

AFTER DELIVERING ACKERMAN TO JACOBS and satiating him with a stack of cash, Hawk headed south on the Bo-Kenema Highway toward the border. Jacobs, who promised to keep Ackerman safe, proceeded to give Hawk a brief overview of the rail line located on the Liberian side of the Manu River. Primarily used for transporting mined elements to Monrovia for process and shipment, the Manu River Railway provided the safest route for Demby. The direct route and lack of regular civilian passengers meant Demby or his men were assured of reaching their destination with little or no threat of robbery.

According to Jacobs, the train left the Manu station daily at midnight.

"That gives you three hours or maybe four. This is Africa," Jacobs said. He concluded his directions by telling Hawk how to slip across the Manu River undetected by the Liberian army.

Hawk rushed to his vehicle, hoping to arrive on time. He used the long bumpy drive to formulate a plan for seizing the diamonds and get an update from Alex.

"Alex, how are you on this fine evening?" he said,

starting the phone conversation.

"Better than you, I'm sure."

"I don't know. Have you been whipped and shot at in the past six hours?"

"Let me think while I sip on my latte. Hmmm. Nope. My biggest conflict in the last six hours was making sure some rude businessman didn't steal my cab. I'm pretty sure, my evening is going better than yours."

"Great. I was hoping so. I also wanted to tell you that I'm not sure the missiles are here. If they are, Demby's team has done a pretty good job of hiding them."

"Keep looking. Blunt swears they're there somewhere."

"Will do, but I've got more pressing matters to attend to at the moment."

***

FIVE MINUTES TO MIDNIGHT, Hawk pulled up to the station. There was little activity around the rail yard. A few men trudged past Hawk and hopped onto a flatbed truck that already had at least a dozen men in the back. Then Hawk heard a sound that made him panic.

The train on the track at least fifty meters away

wooshed, releasing its breaks and chugging forward.

Hawk broke into a sprint, going largely ignored by the workers still scattered on the grounds. As he reached the platform, the train was clear by ten meters and gaining speed. Hawk didn't hesitate, leaping off the platform and racing after the train on the track. And after twenty seconds of hard running, he caught up with the final car and grabbed onto it before pulling himself up.

One by one, Hawk shimmied between the two-dozen cars trailing the engine until he found one that contained a pair of Demby's henchmen.

Look what we have here.

It was dark, but he could make out at least one familiar face. One of the men was holding a briefcase. The other pulled a gun, training it on Hawk.

Hawk put up his hands in a gesture of surrender. "Sorry. I don't want any trouble."

He noticed a hatch above the two men had been left open. Backing slowly out of the door, he scaled the outer portion of the car before climbing on top. He peered through the hatch and could make out silhouettes of the men.

Here it goes.

He jumped feet first through the hatch, surprising the men as they tumbled to the ground. Hawk immobilized the one with the gun first, kicking the weapon out of the man's hand before shoving him out the door.

The guard holding the briefcase drew his weapon and prepared to shoot Hawk before he dove to the ground and caught the man off guard. Hawk ripped his knife out of his pocket and slung it at the guard, hitting him square in the chest. The guard clutched the knife before dropping his weapon and collapsing.

Five minutes into the trip, Hawk had gained possession of the diamonds, but he needed to exit immediately. He grabbed the handle of the suitcase and peered into the Liberian jungle, lit only by a pale moon. With each passing second, Hawk realized it would make his journey back to his car and then to Koidu that much longer. He needed to jump soon.

Hawk stuck his head out of the car and peered into the dark forest surrounding the train. He noticed a small clearing up ahead that looked like it would make for a safe landing spot. Hugging the briefcase, he jumped.

Hawk landed hard, rolling for at least twenty meters before coming to a stop. With at least an hour hike ahead of him, Hawk first stopped and removed the diamonds from the briefcase. He shoved them into his pocket and began his journey back toward the station to his vehicle.

***

IT WAS NEARLY 2:00 a.m. when Hawk returned to his Forerunner and headed north on the Bo-Kenema Highway. He jammed his foot on the gas and called Alex. After debriefing her on the details of the mission, he decided to delve into other matters with her for his long drive back to Yokodu.

"Talk to me, Alex," he said.

"What do you want to know about?"

"It's just past two here, and I'm about to fall asleep. Anything that will keep me awake will suffice."

"What about my love life?"

"I said anything that will keep me awake."

"Apparently being a bad ass operative doesn't suppress your sardonic wit."

Hawk chuckled. "What can I say? I possess many skills."

"Not sure I have much interesting to say about my love life, but there are some other interesting developments taking place right now."

"Go on."

"I'd rather save this type of conversation for when we meet in person."

"And break protocol again?"

Alex sighed. "Since when did you suddenly start caring about following all the rules?"

"Good point."

"Yes, but I'm still failing miserably at coming up with a conversation to keep you awake."

"Mulling over what you can't say might suffice, though if it doesn't work, it's not like I can pull into a convenience store and grab a Red Bull for the ride."

"You know where to find me if that doesn't work."

"There is one thing you can tell me."

Alex's voice perked up. "What's that?"

"Have you been able to find those missiles with any satellite imaging?"

"Nope. Not a thing. I'm beginning to wonder if that was bad intel."

"Maybe, but there are some questionable characters here."

"Hawk, you're in godforsaken Sierra Leone. The chances of you finding any person who *doesn't* have questionable character are slim to none."

"There are a few here who seem to be more than your run of the mill riffraff."

"What about that tracking device Colton gave you?"

"Nothing so far," Hawk said as he shifted in his seat and rubbed his eyes. "I wonder if he's got a problem with his tracker."

"Well, at least you got the diamonds."

"I doubt Blunt will be satisfied with that."

"Just be careful, Hawk, okay?"

"It's hard to be careful when you're committed."

He ended the call and rubbed the corner of his eyes again. A shot of caffeine would be nice, but there were plenty of other things to think about, starting with the issue of Ackerman's health. For some reason, he couldn't stop thinking about how he left her.

***

WHEN HAWK RETURNED to Yokodu around 6:00 a.m., he needed to stash the diamonds some-where safe for leverage. Keeping them on his person created a more dangerous situation, one where he could be simply robbed at gunpoint and the fruits of his hard work would vanish. He found a spot about a mile from the outfitters just off the side of the road. Hawk dug a small hole and buried the sack at the base of a tree, which he marked by carving a design on it with a knife.

When Hawk pulled into the outfitters parking lot, he noticed a light in the lobby was still on. Before going to his room, he stopped in to see if anyone was milling around. He'd already decided that he was going to sleep in a different room, talk to an employee of the mine about the missiles, and embark on one final search for them before concluding his unfinished business with Demby.

After calling out several times with no reply, Hawk slipped behind the counter and grabbed a key to another room. He'd almost disappeared before he heard Ethan Jacobs calling for him.

"Brady Hawk, is that you?" Jacobs asked.

Hawk spun around and saw Jacobs standing in the doorway behind the counter. "How's Dr. Ackerman?"

"She's fine. Just a flesh wound. I got her patched up."

"Thanks for doing that."

Jacobs smiled. "My pleasure." He paused. "She told me that she wanted to see you whenever you returned, no matter what time it was."

Hawk glanced up at the clock behind the counter. "It's late."

"She emphasized *any time*. And to be honest, I doubt she's gone to sleep since you left. She was worried sick about you."

"Fine. I'll poke my head in to see if she's awake."

"Room eleven at the end of the hall."

Hawk nodded and meandered toward Ackerman's door. It was cracked, and he knocked softly before pushing it open.

Instead of seeing her propped up in bed, she was gagged and tied to a chair.

"Doc?" he said as he rushed in.

She writhed in her seat, trying to get his attention. But it was too late.

Demby, who'd been hiding in a corner of the room, slammed the door shut and trained his gun on Hawk.

"Easy there, Mr. Martin—or whatever the hell your name is," Demby said. "Keep those hands where I can see them, and slowly turn around."

Hawk complied, raising his hands in the air.

"I heard what you did to my men on the train. Quite impressive. But now I hold the upper hand. Don't make this any more difficult than it has to be."

"What do you want?" Hawk asked.

"It's simple. I want an exchange—the diamonds for the doctor."

CHAPTER 35

BLUNT SLICED INTO HIS SLAB of crispy pork at the Blue Duck Tavern, his favorite Beltway restaurant. He dreamed about hiring a personal chef who could cook that well and serve his favorite dish on the menu everyday. He was convinced he'd never grow tired of pork. The waiter slipped up to the table and asked Blunt if he was satisfied with how his meal tasted.

"Just rename this dish *mana*," Blunt said, "because this has to be straight from Heaven."

The waiter nodded. "I'll pass your compliments on to the chef."

"Pass on my compliments? Hell, I wanna hire the man."

Blunt guided another succulent piece of meat into his mouth and took his time eating every last morsel. He was finished and waiting on his banana cream pie for dessert when his phone buzzed.

Cursing under his breath, Blunt answered his

phone, speaking in hushed tones.

"Please tell me the world isn't falling apart again," Blunt said.

"The situation has changed since we last spoke."

Blunt sighed and put his elbows on the table before leaning forward. "What is it this time? Hawk?"

"Yes, he's run into a bit of a roadblock."

"A bit of one? Or one that covers the entire highway?"

"The latter, sir. He's got one hour to return the diamonds or else Demby is going to kill a doctor working with a humanitarian aid project."

"Screw the doctor. Tell him to get outta there. He got what he went for."

"Not exactly."

Blunt stood up and decided to slip outside so he could talk more freely.

"What do you mean, *not exactly*?" Blunt asked as he exited the restaurant.

"What I mean, sir, is that he hasn't retrieved the weapons. And if he leaves now, he won't be able to retrieve them now—or ever, since his cover has likely been blown already."

"I'm not greedy. I'll take what I can get."

"But, sir, you've stressed how important those missiles are. Don't you—?"

"Tell Hawk to get the hell outta there. That's an order."

"Roger that," Alex said. "I think he might need an extraction, too."

Blunt growled. "An extraction? He knows the rules. There'll be no extractions on these missions. He's on his own, and if he can't figure out a way back home, that's his own damn problem."

"So, you're just going to let the diamonds fall back into their hands? Seems like a waste of a good operative to me."

"Save your philosophical waxing for someone who cares," Blunt said before he hung up his phone.

He grabbed the handle and prepared to tug it toward him before he stopped. If he chose to be honest with himself, he knew Alex made sense. It'd be a waste to lose Hawk, not to mention the diamonds.

Blunt turned around and ducked into an alleyway near the restaurant. He dialed the number of General Patrick Stanley and hoped he'd pick up. General Stanley served in the same platoon as Blunt during the Vietnam War but now oversaw a special reconnaissance team in central Africa.

"I rarely answer my phone before I've had my first cup of coffee," Stanley snarled. "Are you sure you want to take that chance for whatever it is that you're about to ask me?"

Blunt stopped and contemplated Stanley's comment for a brief second before moving forward. "If I could wait, I would."

"Bet you thought you'd never play Russian roulette with an American general."

Blunt forced a laugh. "This is serious."

"Lay it on me."

"I've got an operative in Sierra Leone who needs some help."

"What kind of help?"

"The kind that requires more muscle than he has."

"What about your survival of the fittest policy? What happened to that?" Stanley scoffed.

"Policies are made to be broken. But this isn't him—it's about what he's after. And it's in all our best interest if this mission is a success."

"I warned you when this started that I wouldn't help you and—"

"I know—and if it wasn't so important, I wouldn't call you. But this is different."

Stanley took a deep breath and exhaled slowly. "Send the details to my secure email account. I'll take it from there."

"Thanks. You have no idea how much this means to me."

"How can I say *no* to a guy who saved my life?" Stanley paused. "Let's just not make a practice of this, agreed?"

Blunt smiled. "I can live with that."

"Go finish that fancy dinner I imagine you're having at some swanky D.C. restaurant. We'll take care of it from here. I've got a team in Freetown that can handle this, I'm sure."

Blunt ended the call and then called Alex to have her send all the information to Stanley. While Blunt hated being indebted to others, Stanley owed a lifetime of favors. As long as he didn't have to presume upon the general's good graces all the time, Blunt felt more comfortable sending Hawk into dangerous situations.

But Blunt knew the real reason he couldn't let Hawk fail. Letting Alex think that it was her idea to enlist the help of another military black ops team was all part of Blunt's plan. Besides, he couldn't let his top asset fail in the field.

Blunt needed the diamonds—even more than he needed Hawk alive.

CHAPTER 36

HAWK RETURNED TO WHERE HE BURIED the raw diamonds and peered into the small sack he'd retrieved from Demby's henchmen less than twelve hours ago. If forced to make a guess, Hawk estimated the retail value of what he held in his hands was somewhere in the neighborhood of twenty to twenty-five million. It'd finance Al Hasib for several months, though not much more given the rate the organization was burning through its artillery.

These animals will pay one day.

Hawk clutched the sack and surveyed the area nearby, its desolation interrupted only occasionally by a vehicle creeping by and kicking up clouds of dust.

Despite his best efforts under the circumstances, he'd been unable to locate the missiles supposedly hidden by Demby. Hawk ventured back to his vehicle when he noticed Solomon, the young boy whose father he'd rescued a few days ago. Solomon smiled as he caught Hawk staring.

Then Hawk broke into a jog toward the boy.

"Solomon, it's me, Mr. Martin."

The boy smiled and nodded.

Hawk grabbed the boy's arm. "You remember me? From the mine?"

Solomon bobbed his head before breaking into a tribal language Hawk struggled to identify, much less understand.

"Can you show me where you live?" Hawk asked.

Solomon nodded.

At least he understands me.

Hawk ran back to his car and followed Solomon along the road. A few minutes later, the boy led Hawk into a modest home in search of Amad, the boy's father.

"Is your father here?" Hawk asked.

Solomon pointed down the hallway.

Hawk smiled at the boy and headed toward his father's room.

"Amad, do you remember me? Mr. Martin?" Hawk said once he caught a glimpse of the man, who was sitting up in his bed.

Amad nodded. "How could I forget? You saved my life."

"I was just happy to help."

Amad stood up and pulled on a bathrobe, tying it around his waist. "What can I help *you* with, Mr. Martin?"

"I was hoping you could help me find some missiles."

"Missiles?"

Hawk eyed Amad closely. "I think you know what I'm talking about, don't you?"

"Let's suppose I did. Why would I tell you anything about them?"

"Because I'm here to defuse a situation, not enflame it. I don't think you want to carry the burden of the inevitable weight of your guilt."

"And you think Demby will use them?"

Hawk shrugged. "Not sure. But this is the same man who was willing to leave all of you buried in the mines."

Amad shuffled across the room and pulled out a small sheet of paper from his desk. He started scribbling down something. After he finished, he turned and handed the paper to Hawk.

"You should be able to find the missiles here. I saw them one afternoon when I was retrieving some supplies to fix a beam in the mine. They're well hidden, but if he still has them, they're probably still there."

Hawk thanked Amad. "You have no idea how many lives you might have just saved."

"Maybe you saving my life will prove to be worthwhile."

"It's always worthwhile to save any good man,"

Hawk said as he cut his eyes toward Solomon, who'd wandered into the room. "Especially a father like yourself. I can tell you love him."

"I try. I'm all Solomon's got after his mother died from Ebola," Amad said. "We try to stick together."

"Don't stop." Hawk held up the piece of paper. "And thank you again for this information."

***

HAWK SLIPPED A TRACKER into the bag of diamonds and took a deep breath before entering the outpost. With his gun drawn, he entered the facility. Slumped in the corner was Ethan Jacobs, dead with a gunshot to the head. Hawk crept down the hallway, glancing in both directions in an effort to mitigate any surprise attacks. Once he reached the room, he slowly pushed the door open to find Dr. Ackerman still gagged and tied to a chair. Demby hovered over her, jamming his gun into her head.

"The diamonds," Demby said, holding out his hand.

"Let her go," Hawk said. "She's got nothing to do with this."

Demby glared at Hawk. "She has everything to do with this. If she had kept her nose in her own business, this would've been over a long time ago."

"And I'd be dead," Hawk snapped. "But things don't always go like we plan."

Demby flashed a wide grin. "No, they don't. But I always get my way."

"I upheld my end of the bargain. It's time for you to uphold yours."

Demby gestured with his gun for Hawk to move. "Over there. I don't want any surprises."

Hawk complied, maintaining eye contact with Demby while walking across the room.

Demby watched Hawk untie Ackerman. Once Demby finished, he yanked Ackerman up and shoved her toward Hawk.

"Don't get any ideas," Demby said, raising his gun toward them. "If I don't walk out of here with these diamonds, I've instructed my men to lay waste to this building."

Hawk didn't flinch, keeping his gun also trained on Demby.

Demby shuffled toward the exit, never taking his eyes off them. Once he reached the doorway, he used the door as a shield before he opened fire, hitting the doctor in the back.

"Sorry, Doc. Just couldn't take any chances," Demby said before vanishing down the hallway.

Ackerman crumpled to the floor, writhing in pain.

Hawk knelt down to help her, ripping sheets off

the bed and creating a makeshift bandage to stop the bleeding.

"Don't worry about me," she said. "Go get that bastard."

Hawk refused. "Not until you're stable."

"None of my vital organs were hit. It's just a flesh wound."

Hawk pulled the bloodied sheet off her back to peek at the opening, where she continued to hemorrhage blood.

"Are you sure about that?" he asked.

"I'm fine. Go get him."

"I put a tracker in the diamonds."

"He'll be long gone if you wait too long. Besides, I'll get Jacobs to help me."

"Jacobs is dead."

She shook her head. "Figures."

"I'm staying."

"No, you're not. Get your ass out of here, and go make Demby pay. I won't take no for an answer."

Hawk felt uneasy about leaving her, but he knew she was right. Given too much of a head start, Demby could vanish—the diamonds and missiles along with him.

And Hawk wasn't about to let that happen.

CHAPTER 37

ALEX FORWARDED HER CALLS to her cell phone in case Hawk needed her. She figured he was competent enough to complete the mission. Besides, she needed sleep and plenty of it. Yet she wasn't surprised when Hawk called.

"Do you have any idea what time it is here?" she said as she answered.

"Alex, I need your help," Hawk said.

She could hear Hawk's engine roaring and surging in the background.

"Where are you? What's going on?"

"I don't have time to explain everything, but I'm pursuing Musa Demby as we speak. He's got the diamonds."

"How did that happen?"

"I'll tell you all the gory details later, but for now, I need you to follow one of my trackers I put into the sack of diamonds I gave to Demby in an exchange."

"Searching for it now," she said, typing furiously on her keyboard. Only two trackers affiliated with

Hawk were activated, and they were both traveling in the same direction only a few meters apart.

"Tell me you got something."

"I do," Alex said. "It's right in front of you."

"If I lose it, please let me know. I can't afford to have Demby disappear into the jungle."

"I'm on it."

Before Alex could say another word, Hawk let out a string of expletives.

"What is it?" she asked.

"Those bastards must've let the air out of my tires."

Alex was incredulous. "And you're just now figuring this out?"

"I think that was the plan," he said, the background noise dropping from a roar to a low hum. "There aren't any other vehicles around for me to take now. Just keep tracking them. I'm going to need to know how to find them again once I find an alternate mode of transportation."

"Uh, you may not need to," Alex said.

"Why's that?"

"Demby turned left and stopped about a quarter of a mile from your present location."

Hawk chuckled. "Ole Amad wasn't lying to me."

"What's that?"

"I know exactly where I'm going now."

Alex hung up. She wished she could do more to help Hawk with the mission, but if scrambling out of bed in the middle of the night to track a sack of diamonds that could potentially be funding a dangerous terrorist cell was all she could do, she'd do it with pride. Keeping Hawk alive was her top priority.

But finding out what was really going on with Blunt and Searchlight was a close second—and she needed Hawk to help her do it.

CHAPTER 38

DEMBY PARKED HIS SUV in a small clearing in the jungle and dialed a number on his cell phone. Around him, a hive of activity began with the simple wave of his hand. Armed guards scurried across the jungle floor, preparing several transport vehicles. Deeper in the jungle covered with branches was a truck. Demby scanned the area as he waited for the party on the other end of his call to pick up.

Demby's Al Hasib contact had left him several messages, each one demanding to know if they were still moving forward with the deal. On the final voicemail, the Al Hasib agent sounded irked and impatient.

"Where are the diamonds?" the man said.

Demby sighed. "They're with me. I'll be leaving shortly with them."

"And the missiles?"

"I'm afraid you lost out to a higher bidder."

"We had a deal and—"

"I'm always open to negotiations, and this particular client doubled your price."

"Karif Fazil won't be happy about this."

Demby chuckled. "And what's he going to do about it? I am, after all, the only way he's able to liquidate assets without getting caught."

The agent wasn't amused. "Don't underestimate Fazil. He will take your mine if he wants to."

"I'd like to see him try."

"Will you be at the drop-off point in an hour?"

"Yes."

"Good. Don't be late."

Demby hung up and watched the men busily preparing for the trip ahead with one of the smaller trucks, while another team uncovered the missile transport truck and gassed it up. In one fell swoop, he was going to make not one but two big scores. Once he got his money, he had no intention of ever spending another day at Sefadu Holdings. He'd pay someone else to manage day-to-day operations while he lived it up on a beach somewhere. He'd heard the Caribbean was a nice place to live.

However, he refused to let himself smile, even though the urge was almost overwhelming. He wasn't going to relax until he had the money in his bank account and was flying over the ocean.

Demby still had a long way to go.

CHAPTER 39

HAWK PULLED A LOW-HANGING BRANCH to the side and studied the camp that apparently served as the base of operations for Demby's other enterprises. A thin veil of fog settled over the jungle canopy as midmorning rays of sunlight speckled the ground. Munitions and weapons were stacked in crates six feet high on one side of the camp; a loaded missile transport truck sat parked on the other. Visser leaned up against the missile truck along with Soto and Perryman.

How come I'm not surprised?

In the two minutes he'd spent observing, Hawk concocted a rough plan of attack. But he never had the chance to enact it.

Hawk whipped his head in the direction of a covered flatbed truck that roared to life. Demby stood nearby and barked orders. Hawk couldn't make out everything that was said, but he heard enough to know what was on board.

Without hesitating, Hawk broke into a dead sprint, managing to stay parallel to the truck and using the thick vegetation to stay hidden from the guards patrolling the area. Upon entering the compound, Hawk discovered that Demby used a camouflaged fence for security purposes. If Hawk's calculations were right, he'd have enough time to jump into the back of the empty flatbed truck when it slowed to get through the gate.

Hawk panted as he crouched down, waiting for his moment to strike. The truck came to a halt before one of the guards opened the gate to allow passage. Once the vehicle reached the main road, the guard secured the gate and hustled back to the cab. That was Hawk's cue.

He dashed after the truck, this time clambering aboard the flatbed of the transport vehicle as it lurched forward while the driver shifted gears. Refraining from taking immediate action in order to avoid the possibility of Demby's men happening up on them, Hawk didn't move for a couple of minutes. In his mind, he visualized every punch he was about to throw, every kick he was about to deliver. He never saw himself losing.

With a deep breath, Hawk initiated his plan. His first challenge was to scale the outside of the truck in order to gain access to the cab. He'd almost made it to the cab when he saw the door spring open and a guard turn to take aim. Anticipating the move, Hawk kicked the gun out of the man's hands before swinging into the cab.

Hawk kicked the man in the face before wrapping his feet around the man's head. Hawk twisted until he heard the man's neck snap. Flinging the guard's body out of the truck, Hawk looked up to see the driver training a gun on him.

The driver took aim and fired a shot, hitting Hawk in the left shoulder. When the driver went for a second shot, the gun jammed. Then the driver pulled out a large knife and waved it in Hawk's direction.

"Out—now, or else I stop this truck and carve you up," the driver said, gesturing for Hawk to exit the cab. "I didn't get the nickname 'The Butcher' on accident."

The driver was so focused on Hawk that he didn't have time to prepare for the pothole that jarred both men when the front tires slammed it at sixty kilometers per hour.

Seizing the opportunity created when The Butcher's knife slipped out of his hand, Hawk lunged for the steering wheel and jerked it hard to the right. The man resisted admirably, landing a few punches on Hawk but failing to regain control of the steering wheel.

As the truck rumbled along, Hawk edged it closer

to the trees lining the left side of the road. Once they got close enough, Hawk grabbed the steering wheel and used it as leverage to jam his feet into The Butcher's rib cage, prying lose his hands. Then Hawk used his foot to reach across The Butcher and open the driver's side door. Hawk followed up with another kick that sent The Butcher flying out of the cab and into a tree. Even above the roar of the engine, Hawk could hear the thud and cracking of the man's ribs.

That ought to take care of him.

Hawk gained control of the vehicle before stomping on the brakes. He rifled through the glove box in search of the diamonds.

Nothing.

He checked a toolbox underneath the passenger's seat.

No diamonds.

Hawk pounded the steering wheel with his fist. He knew he didn't imagine them being there.

"Looking for these?" came a voice from behind Hawk.

Hawk spun around to see the driver holding up the sack of diamonds.

"I'll take that now," Hawk said.

"Over my dead body," the man said as he staggered toward Hawk.

Without waiting another second, the man shoved

the diamonds into his pocket and rushed Hawk.

Hawk needed only two hits to incapacitate the man, hitting him once in the neck before delivering a punishing blow to the face. Hawk jostled behind The Butcher and quickly snapped his neck.

The Butcher collapsed onto the ground. Hawk yanked the diamonds out of the man's pocket and stared at the limp body beneath him.

"Words have meanings, mate," Hawk said, mocking the fresh corpse. "Next time try not to be so literal, okay?"

Hawk rushed back to the truck and drove back toward the camp, crashing through the camouflaged fence and storming into the staging area of the compound. In need of a high-powered weapon, he slammed on the brakes and skidded the truck to a stop in front of the munitions. The truck served as a cover for him to arm himself and as a bunker to fight from.

Beneath a hail of bullets, Hawk scrambled to find the right weapon and get it operational. It took twenty seconds—twenty agonizingly long seconds—to get armed and start fighting.

Using one of the AK-47s in the crates, Hawk started methodically picking off Soto and Perryman along with the half dozen remaining guards. However, Hawk realized he hadn't killed all of them: Visser and Demby remained.

On the other side of the camp, the missile transport truck fired up with Visser occupying the driver's seat and Demby assembling a rocket launcher in the cab next to him.

Oh, hell, no. I'm not getting on another moving vehicle today.

Hawk ran toward them and peppered the cab with his machine gun.

Visser seemed unfazed and drove ahead.

Careful not to destroy the missiles, Hawk raced back toward the weapons cache and opened a grenade launcher. All he needed to do was disable the truck, confident he could handle Visser and Demby on the ground.

Working quickly to assemble the launcher, Hawk kept one eye on the truck, which was on the cusp of exiting the camp when he saw it surprisingly come to a stop.

It must be Christmas.

Hawk raced in the direction of the truck, staying low in the vegetation surrounding the camp. If they hadn't seen him, he'd have the element of surprise on his side as well as plenty of trees to take cover in if they came after him.

Demby jumped out of the cab, his feet hitting the ground with a solid thud.

"Come on out, Mr. Martin," Demby said, toting a rocket launcher. "I have a surprise for you."

Hawk bit his lip, unwilling to give up his location over a childish taunt. Maneuvering through the bushes to get a plain view of the front of the truck, Hawk steadied his launcher and fired. The grenade hit the right front portion of the cab, setting off an explosion that started a small fire. Demby suffered an indirect and lay motionless five meters away from the initial point of impact.

While scanning the area for Visser, Hawk heard a motorcycle kick start before he saw it rumbling along the road toward the exit. Still out of sight, Hawk waited for the right moment and then heaved a large stone at the front tire of Visser's bike. Upon contact with the rock, the bike wobbled. Visser overcompensated and lay the bike down.

Hawk didn't want to take any chances with Visser, putting two bullets in Visser's chest and another one in his head before returning focus to Demby.

By the time Hawk reached Demby, the fire at the front of the truck was raging. Crawling toward the trees for a safe haven, Demby struggled. And Hawk had no interest in extending the monster any mercy.

He used his foot to roll Demby onto his back. Bruised and bleeding, Demby was in no shape to fight. But Hawk made sure Demby heard a final lecture before putting him out of his misery.

Demby looked up at Hawk but said nothing.

Hawk pulled out the sack of diamonds and dangled them in the air.

"I know these may just look like regular diamonds to you, but I'll tell you what these diamonds really do," Hawk said. "They murder and maim innocent children. They lead to the death and destruction of families and livelihoods and nations—and all so you can get your cut. You disgust me."

Hawk shook his head and glanced around the compound to make sure no one else was moving. They weren't.

"Now, I'm going to do what you should've done to me when you had the chance—kill me quickly." Hawk trained his gun on Demby, who cowered behind both of his hands.

Hawk pulled the trigger, emptying three shots into Demby.

"By the way, my name's not Martin—it's Hawk."

CHAPTER 40

BLUNT'S FEET RHYTHMICALLY POUNDED the treadmill in his downstairs gym. Locked away in his fortress in a posh enclave in McLean, he considered his home a safe haven, untouchable by anyone in the outside world, cordial or nefarious. Home was the only place he wanted to be while he sorted out what was going on. His position within The Chamber seemed tenuous at best as he was unsure whom in the group he could trust. Perhaps Lord Williams acted alone or he was acting on orders from the group wielding the most power. Blunt needed answers; he needed a plan.

The sun had crested the towering pines that covered the back of his hilly lot, which stretched to the edge of Bullneck Run Creek. Blunt finished his workout and put on a pot of coffee while he pondered a path that didn't result in his death. When he decided to first engage with The Chamber and become their inside guy in D.C., he knew this was a possible eventual outcome, though he never wanted to admit it. The money proved to be a helpful perk, but the power intoxicated him. He'd been around D.C. long enough to know that whoever sat in the Oval Office was nothing more than a puppet. Democrat, Republican—it didn't matter. Those leaders immortalized in the history books did the bidding of special interest groups. Blunt learned it was all an illusion. The real power rested with those who operated outside the bounds of archaic documents and tired unified organizations like the U.S. Constitution and the U.N. Security Council. And Blunt enjoyed exercising such power.

He broke out of his trance when his phone buzzed on the kitchen counter. Blunt poured a cup of coffee and took a sip before answering.

If I could just stay here and drink the world's finest coffee every day . . .

"This is Blunt," he said as he answered his phone.

It was Hawk, who proceeded to give the run down on everything that had just happened, including seizing the weapons and taking control of the diamonds.

"Great. Bury the diamonds and then send me the location. Also include the coordinates for the missiles. I'll arrange to have someone pick them all up."

"You sure you want to leave that to chance?" Hawk asked. "I just left a high body count here. Who's to say that more men aren't on their way?"

"This isn't a discussion."

"I know I can sneak the diamonds back. You'll have no way of verifying if you've been stiffed or not."

"Just follow my orders, Hawk. You've done all that I've asked you to do and more. It's time to get you back home."

Blunt hung up and proceeded to dial General Patrick.

"The package is almost ready," Blunt said. "I'm sending you the coordinates for the pickup in just a few minutes."

"You're going to owe me big time," Patrick said.

"How about we call it even after this is all over with? Besides, you're going to be a hero for seizing back those stolen missiles right from underneath the terrorist's noses."

"It'll be a lie."

"Some lies are worth being told and repeated. Your career will thank you for it."

"Quite frankly, I'm just hoping I don't regret it."

Blunt took another sip of his coffee. "All you have to do for me is return a small sack of diamonds, no questions asked. Think you can do that?"

"Why would I ever ask you a question in the first place? I never get straight answers."

"I'll take that as a yes."

"We'll await your instructions."

Blunt pumped his fist. "Excellent. I'll be in touch."

He hung up the phone and, for the first time in several years, started to dream about the future. He had hope that not only could he resolve his issues with The Chamber, but that he could *thrive* within their structure—or maybe shed them altogether.

Blunt sent out an email to request a meeting with one of The Chamber's agents. The request was readily accepted. Blunt had plenty of questions that needed to be answered, including who was the hacker named Bare Bones and was he or she affiliated with anyone in The Chamber. If he could get all his questions answered, he might be able to make sense of what was happening and forge a path forward.

The fog of fear and uncertainty started to lift as he grew confident he'd find out what he needed to know.

He lit a cigar and jammed it into his mouth. The last loose end he needed to tie up was the affair with Liam Jepsen. Blunt still hadn't heard back from Thor, though he didn't have to in order to know that Jepsen was still alive. Without a peep uttered about it on the news, it was clear nothing had happened. Blunt would have to chase down his operative and find out what was causing the delay tomorrow.

But for now, Blunt was back.

CHAPTER 41

TWO DAYS AFTER RETURNING from Sierra Leone, Hawk settled into a booth in the back of the cafe at The National Archives facility in College Park. He was anxious to hear what Alex refused to tell him over the phone. If he was honest with himself, he'd grown quite fond of her since they started working together. The feeling of being attracted to a woman seemed foreign to him after he bitterly swore off romance following Emily's death. But the feeling in his chest seemed strangely familiar the moment Alex walked around the corner.

Hawk stood up and greeted her with a hug, the first time he'd made such a bold move.

"Don't you look nice," Hawk said, gesturing for her to have a seat. "I got you a coffee. Are you hungry?"

"No, thanks. I'm going out to eat tonight with a friend."

Hawk cocked his head to one side. "A friend?

What kind of friend?"

"Just a guy friend who helped me out with some work-related projects. No big deal."

"So, you've got a date?"

"Heaven help us if K-Squared thinks it's an actual date."

"Wait—the guy's name is K-Squared?"

"He's a hacker and—"

Hawk held up his hand. "You don't need to say anything else. Hackers inhabit their own ethos that I don't care to enter into."

"Me either, but sometimes you have to take one for the team."

"Well, that's a shame because I was going to see if you want to watch *Mughal-E-Azam* with me tonight? It's one of my favorites and playing at the Georgetown Theater for Bollywood Week."

"One of my favorites, too. Now I'm wondering if I can avoid taking one for the team."

Hawk chuckled and leaned forward. "So, what's this big secret that you couldn't tell me on the phone?"

Alex glanced around the room. She and Hawk were the only two people in the cafe, but she still leaned in close, speaking in a hushed voice.

"When I broke into The Vault at CIA headquarters, your father's file was empty."

"Figures," Hawk said. "They've been trying to hide

everything from me. Is that what you wanted to tell me?"

"Oh, no. There's more. Being the snoopy person that I am, I ventured over to your last name and looked up your file."

"And?"

"It was packed, and I didn't get to read it all but—"

"Out with it, Alex. You're killing me."

She smiled. "But I read several pages about the CIA's attempted recruitment of you."

Hawk looked at her incredulously. "The CIA never tried to recruit me. And as far as I know, the CIA doesn't even know about Firestorm."

"Well, you're wrong. They tried on several occasions, but you rebuffed them."

"I don't ever recall being approached by anyone."

"There were several records of interactions different agents had with you after Emily's death."

Hawk leaned back in his seat and furrowed his brow. "They used Emily's death as a tool to recruit me?"

Alex shrugged. "Not sure. What I thought was interesting is that the report never referred to her death but instead as *The Thornton incident.*"

"What do you think that means?"

"I have no idea, but I thought it was curious for sure."

Hawk sighed. "Just another thing I need to ask Blunt about." He paused. "By the way, thanks again for your help on the mission in Sierra Leone."

"So, it was a rousing success?"

"An Al Hasib funding pipeline was eliminated along with other underworld characters."

"That's always a good thing."

"And I got to help some people."

"When you rescued them from a mine?"

Hawk smiled. "Yes, but that wasn't the only thing. I deeded the mine to Amad, one of the workers I pulled out from beneath the rubble. He was a single dad who helped me out."

"How'd you pull that off?"

"I killed Demby, the Sefadu Holdings owner, and went back and found the deed to the land and business—and I transferred it over into Amad's name."

"I guess we can add forgery to your skill set."

"Got my start in elementary school by writing notes from my mom to cover all the times I played hooky."

"You were an agent in training all the way back then."

He laughed. "I've still got plenty to learn—including how to research better and pull on those threads until the ball of lies unravels."

"Keep tugging," Alex said as she glanced at her

watch. "Gotta run. I'll be in touch."

Hawk grabbed Alex's wrist and smiled as he looked up at her. "Have fun writing code tonight."

She rolled her eyes and left.

***

THE NEXT MORNING, Hawk tugged his hoodie over his head and sat on the steps of the Lincoln Memorial overlooking the reflecting pool. He adjusted his sunglasses, pressing them further up on the bridge of his nose as the water shimmered. It was the perfect spot to contemplate everything happening around him and to him.

He had plenty to smile about in the midst of the chaos. Amad and Solomon would have a chance to make a better life for themselves and the people around them. Blunt had managed to find an anonymous donor to supply Dr. Ackerman with all the resources she'd ever need to continue operating SLAM. And Al Hasib was going to have a more difficult time financing its operation.

But Hawk still felt unsettled. He had a thousand questions for Blunt, starting with Hawk's father. How did his father die? Or was he really dead yet? What happened that led to his death? Hawk also had questions for Blunt regarding his involvement in everything around Hawk's recruitment. Was Emily still alive? Was she a plant?

But it was the questions he couldn't ask Blunt that nagged Hawk the most: Was Blunt dirty?

Hawk hadn't even sorted them out in his own head when he caught the smell of a cigar wafting on the wind. He didn't even move before he began speaking.

"Smoking those second-rate cigars is going to not only kill you with cancer but it's also going to make it impossible for you to sneak up on someone," Hawk said. "If you were a real spy, you'd know that."

Blunt sat down next to Hawk on the steps and stared off into the distance. "I only do this so we don't have to engage in a formal greeting before we begin our conversation."

"For a man of such means, you really have no taste in cigars," Hawk said.

"I could say the same for your taste in scotch."

Hawk took a deep breath. "Your smoking is the last thing I have a beef with you about."

"Go on."

"For starters, did you know the CIA was actively trying to recruit me after the Peace Corps?"

"I heard rumors, yes."

"What about *before* the Peace Corps?"

"Your skill set makes you an attractive recruit. It's why I sought you out."

"Was Emily a plant?"

"What did you say?"

Hawk narrowed his eyes. "You heard me. Was Emily a plant? Is she still alive?"

Blunt appeared taken aback by the line of questioning. "Not to my knowledge. If she's not, someone played a cruel and twisted joke on you."

"Will you find out for me?"

Blunt put his hands up. "Look, I don't know all the CIA's dirty business, and I don't think I could get certain things out of them either. But I'll ask around. If I hear something, I'll let you know." He paused. "Any other burning questions you have for me?"

"Yeah, the one that burns in my mind almost a dozen times a day—what happened to my father? The real one, not the guy you people have been trotting out as my replacement dad? What happened to him?"

"Your father was a good man, one of the best agents I've ever known in this business. But sometimes even the best men have a challenging time standing up to the evil powers that operate above the law."

"So, what are you trying to say? What did he do?"

"What I mean is that—" Blunt stopped and started to gasp for his breath.

"Senator! Senator!" Hawk put his hands on Blunt and tried to gently shake him out of the trance he appeared to be going into. Each time Hawk called his name, his voice grew louder. "Senator! Talk to me!"

While intensely focused on Blunt, Hawk could hear a small crowd beginning to gather around him. He kept his head down as he pleaded with people to stop filming on their phones and call 9-1-1.

Within five minutes, paramedics rushed onto the scene and hoisted Blunt onto the stretcher. During that period of time, Blunt hadn't changed. His eyes remained opened and glazed over.

"What's going on?" Hawk asked one of the paramedics. "Is he going to be all right?"

"I don't know, sir," the paramedic replied, gently pushing Hawk backward. "Please step away and let us do our job."

Hawk hovered over the medical professionals while they tested and prodded Blunt. Within thirty seconds, they were preparing to push the senator toward their ambulance.

Hawk rushed over and got down close to Blunt's ear, whispering as they rushed toward the vehicle. "Damn it, Senator, don't die on me. I need you to make it. I need answers about who I am."

Hawk tried to climb aboard.

One of the paramedics held out his hand. "Sorry, sir. Family only."

"I'm the only family he's got," Hawk protested.

The paramedic ignored Hawk and closed the door.

The driver then roared away, turning on the sirens that echoed through the D.C. morning air. The wailing ambulance sounded the same to most people—another emergency vehicle trying to save someone. To Hawk, the siren sounded more ominous. Most importantly, Blunt's life hung in the balance. But so did Hawk's answer.

Don't die on me yet.

CHAPTER 42

HANDS CLASPED TOGETHER in front of him, Hawk watched the casket of Senator J.D. Blunt lowered into the ground. He didn't move with the rest of the mourners, who started to head back to their vehicles. A chorus of sorrowful cries from Blunt's ex-wives and former girlfriends provided a sad soundtrack carried by the wind whipping through Arlington Cemetery. It faded softly until Hawk was left alone with his thoughts.

He simultaneously liked and loathed Blunt, though Hawk felt more of the latter in recent days. Blunt's refusal to tell Hawk the truth about his father created a tidal wave of bitterness, one that crashed around Hawk as he looked at the mound of dirt waiting to be shoveled on top of the senator's casket. It was a simple request, yet Blunt refused to honor it. At least, Blunt refused to honor it in a reasonable amount of time. And time had run out.

The longer Hawk stared at the overturned earth,

the angrier he got.

"He's not coming back, if that's what you're thinking," came a familiar voice behind him.

Hawk spun around to see Tom Colton.

"What do you want?"

"Just came to offer my condolences. I know what Senator Blunt meant to you, son," Colton answered.

Hawk felt his face get flushed, not out of embarrassment but out of rage.

"Cut the shenanigans, *Tom*. You're not my father."

Colton cocked his head to one side. "Now, Son, I know you're angry, but is that any way to treat your old man."

"What? The old man who was never there for me? The old man who isn't even my old man? The old man who is so stupid that he'll believe anything he's told or do anything he's told just to hold onto his precious government contracts."

Colton scowled. "I don't know what you've been told, but I sure as hell won't sit around and listen to you talk to me like that. It's obvious that you're letting your emotions get the best of you. I'm going to walk away now and let you cool off."

"Please walk away and never come back," Hawk said.

Hawk returned his gaze to Blunt's plot and continued to sulk. The man in the grave may have given

Hawk a job that filled him with purpose, but that was only after Blunt nearly stripped every chance Hawk had of discovering who his father really was. Hawk didn't have "daddy issues;" he had Blunt issues. And Hawk had to resign himself right then that they'd never be resolved.

After a few more minutes of standing over the grave, Hawk felt a tap on his shoulder. He turned around to see General Johnson.

"I know it goes against protocol for us to meet out in public," Johnson said.

"It's what I was doing with Blunt when he suffered his stroke. Some rules are meant to be broken."

"And some teams are never meant to be broken up," Johnson said as he handed Hawk a piece of paper.

"What's this?" Hawk said.

"It's your next assignment."

"Assignment?"

Johnson smiled and nodded. "Firestorm isn't going anywhere. Just because Blunt is dead doesn't mean there aren't terrorists that need to be stopped out there. Hawk, your government needs you—even if it barely knows you exist."

"And Alex?"

"She's in too. All the details are there, but you'll be briefed more fully once you arrive."

"Where am I headed this time?"

"San Francisco. Talk to you soon."

Johnson tipped his cap and left Hawk alone again.

Blunt may have been gone, but Hawk remained determined to find the answers to all his questions. They were out there. That much he was sure of. He just needed to figure out where to look.

THE END